HOW
IT
HAPPENED

KATE LANGLEY BOSHER

1st WORLD
LIBRARY
Literary Society

How It Happened

Kate Langley Bosher

© 1st World Library – Literary Society, 2004
PO Box 2211
Fairfield, IA 52556
www.1stworldlibrary.org
First Edition

LCCN: 2005901342

Softcover ISBN: 1-4218-1157-X
Hardcover ISBN: 1-4218-1057-3
eBook ISBN: 1-4218-1257-6

Purchase *"How It Happened"*
as a traditional bound book at:
www.1stWorldLibrary.org/purchase.asp?ISBN=1-4218-1157-X

1st World Library Literary Society is a nonprofit
organization dedicated to promoting literacy by:

- Creating a free internet library accessible from any
computer worldwide.
- Hosting writing competitions and offering book
publishing scholarships.

How It Happened
contributed by Tim, Ed & Rodney
in support of
1st World Library Literary Society

TO

MY FAITHFUL FRIEND
ARIADNE ELIZABETH VAUGHAN LATHAM

CHAPTER I

Head on the side and chin uptilted, she held it at arm's-length, turning it now in one direction, now in another, then with deliberation she laid it on the floor.

"I have wanted to do it ever since you were sent me; now I am going to."

Hands on hips, she looked down on the high-crown, narrow-brim hat of stiff gray felt which was at her feet, and nodded at it with firmness and decision. "It's going to be my Christmas present to myself - getting rid of you. Couldn't anything give me as much pleasure as smashing you is going to give. Good-by -"

Raising her right foot, Carmencita held it poised for a half-moment over the hated hat, then with long-restrained energy she brought it down on the steeple-crown and crushed it into shapelessness. "I wish she could see you now." Another vigorous punch was given, then with a swift movement the battered bunch of dull grayness, with its yellow bird and broken buckle of tarnished steel, was sent in the air, and as it landed across the room the child laughed gaily, ran toward it, and with the tip of her toes tossed it here and there. Sending it now up to the ceiling, now toward the mantel, now kicking it over the table, and now to the top of the window, she danced round and round the room, laughing breathlessly. Presently she stooped, picked it up, stuck it on her head, and, going to the stove, opened its top, and with a shake of her curls dropped the once haughty and now humbled head-gear in the fire and watched it burn with joyous satisfaction.

"The first time she wore it we called her Coachman Cattie, it was so stiff and high and hideous, and nobody but a person like her would ever have bought it. I never thought it would some day come to me. Some missioners are nice, some very nice, but some -"

With emphasis the lid of the stove was put back, and, going to the table in the middle of the room, Carmencita picked up the contents of the little work-basket, which had been knocked over in her rushing round, and put them slowly in place. "Some missioners seem to think because you're poor everything God put in other people's hearts and minds and bodies and souls He left out of you. Of course, if you haven't a hat you ought to be thankful for any kind." The words came soberly, and the tiniest bit of a quiver twisted the lips of the protesting mouth. "You oughtn't to know whether it is pretty or ugly or becoming or - You ought just to be thankful and humble, and I'm not either. I don't like thankful, humble people; I'm afraid of them."

Leaving the table where for a minute she had jumbled needles and thread and scissors and buttons in the broken basket, she walked slowly over to the tiny mirror hung above a chest of drawers, and on tiptoes nodded at the reflection before her - nodded and spoke to it.

"You're a sinner, all right, Carmencita Bell, and there's no natural goodness in you. You hate hideousness, and poorness, and other people's cast-offs, and emptiness in your stomach, and living on the top floor with crying babies and a drunken father underneath, and counting every stick of wood before you use it. And you get furious at times because your father is blind and people have forgotten about his beautiful music, and you want chicken and cake when you haven't even enough bacon and bread. You're a sinner, all right. If you were in a class of them you would be at the head. It's the only thing you'd ever be at the head of. You know you're poverty-poor, and still you're always fighting inside, always making out that it is just for a little while. Why don't you -"

The words died on her lips, and suddenly the clear blue eyes, made for love and laughter and eager for all that is lovely in life, dimmed with hot tears, and with a half-sob she turned and threw herself face downward on the rug-covered cot on the opposite side of the room.

"O God, please don't let Father know!" The words came in tones that were terrified. "Please don't ever let him know! I wasn't born good, and I hate bad smells, and dirty things, and ugly clothes, and not enough to eat, but until I am big enough to go to work please, *please* help me to keep Father from knowing! Please help me!"

With a twisting movement the child curled herself into a little ball, and for a moment tempestuous sobbing broke the stillness of the room, notwithstanding the knuckles of two little red hands which were pressed to the large sweet mouth. Presently she lifted the hem of her skirt and wiped her eyes, then she got up.

"I wish I could cry as much as I want to. I never have had a place convenient to do it all by myself, and there's never time, but it gets the choked things out and makes you feel much better. I don't often want to, just sometimes, like before Christmas when you're crazy to do a lot of things you can't do - and some people make you so mad! If I'd been born different and not minding ugly things and loving pretty ones, I wouldn't have hated that hat so. That's gone, anyhow. I've been wanting to see how high I could kick it ever since Miss Cattie sent it to me, and now I've done it. I've got a lot of old clothes I'd like to send to Ballyhack, but I can't send."

She stopped, smoothed her rumpled dress, and shook back the long loose curls which had fallen over her face. "I must be getting sorry for myself. If I am I ought to be spanked. I can't spank, but I can dance. If you don't head it off quick it goes to your liver. I'll head!"

With a swift movement Carmencita sprang across the room and from the mantel took down a once beribboned but now faded and worn tambourine. "You'd rather cry," she said, under her breath, "but you sha'n't cry. I won't let you. Dance! Dance! Dance!"

Aloft the tambourine was shaken, and its few remaining bells broke gaily on the air as with abandon that was bewildering in grace and suppleness the child leaped into movement swift and light and amazing in beauty. Around the room, one arm akimbo, one hand now in the air, now touching with the tambourine the hard, bare floor, now tossing back the loose curls, now waving gaily overhead, faster and faster she danced, her feet in perfect rhythm to the bells; then presently the tambourine was thrown upon the table, and she stopped beside it, face flushed, eyes shining, and breath that came in quick, short gasps.

"That was much better than crying." She laughed. "There isn't much you can do in this world, Carmencita, but you can dance. You've got to do it, too, every time you feel sorry for yourself. I wonder if I could see Miss Frances before I go for Father? I *must* see her. Must! Those Beckwith babies have got the croup, and I want to ask her if she thinks it's awful piggy in me to put all my money, or 'most all, in Father's present. And I want to ask her - I could ask Miss Frances things all night. Maybe the reason I'm not a thankful person is I'm so inquiring. I expect to spend the first hundred years after I get to heaven asking questions."

Going over to the mantel, Carmencita looked at the little clock upon it. "I don't have to go to the wedding-place for father until after six," she said, slowly, "and I'd like to see Miss Frances before I go. If I get there by half past five I can see the people get out of their automobiles and sail in. I wish I could sail somewhere. If I could see some grandness once and get the smell of cabbage and onions out of my nose, which I never will as long as the Rheinhimers live underneath us, I wouldn't mind the other things so much, but there isn't any chance of grandness coming as high up in the air as this. I wonder if God has forgot about us! He has so many to remember -"

With a swift turn of her head, as if listening, Carmencita's eyes grew shy and wistful, then she dropped on her knees by the couch and buried her face in her arms. "If God's forgot I'll remind Him," she said, and tightly she closed her eyes.

"O God" - the words came eagerly, fervently - "we are living in the same place, and every day I hope we will get in a better one, but until we do please help me to keep on making Father think I like it better than any other in town. I thought maybe You had forgotten where we were. I'm too little to go to work yet, and that's why we're still here. We can't pay any more rent, or we'd move. And won't You please let something nice happen? I don't mean miracles, or money, or things like that, but something thrilly and exciting and romantic, if You can manage it. Every day is just the same sort of sameness, and I get so mad-tired of cooking and cleaning and mending, before school and after school and nights, that if something don't happen soon I'm afraid Father will find out what a pretending person I am, and he mustn't find. It's been much better since I knew Miss Frances. I'm awful much obliged to You for letting me know her, but she isn't permanent, Mother McNeil says, and may go away soon. I'm going to try to have a grand Christmas and be as nice as I can to Mrs. Rheinhimer, but she's so lazy and dirty it's hard not to tell her so. And if You could let a nice thing happen for Christmas I hope You will. If it could be a marriage and I could be bridesmaid I'd like that best, as I've never been to an inside wedding, just outside on the street. I don't care for poor marriages. Amen."

On her feet, Carmencita hesitated, then, going to a closet across the room, took from its top shelf a shabby straw hat and put it on. "This was bought for me and fits," she said, as if to some one by her side, "and, straw or no straw, it feels better than that Coachman Cattie, which is gone for evermore. Some day I hope I can burn you up, too" - she nodded to the coat into which she was struggling - "but I can't do it yet. You're awful ugly and much too big, but you're warm and the only one I've got. I'll have half an hour before it's time to go for Father. If Miss Frances is home I can talk a lot in half an hour."

KATE LANGLEY BOSHER

CHAPTER II

Carmencita knocked. There was no answer. She knocked again. After the third knock she opened the door and, hand on the knob, looked in.

"Oh, Miss Frances, I was afraid you had gone out! I knocked and knocked, but you didn't say come in, so I thought I'd look. Please excuse me!"

The girl at the sewing-machine, which was close to the window and far from the door, stopped its running, turned in her chair, and held out her hand. "Hello, Carmencita! I'm glad it's you and not Miss Perkins. I wouldn't want Miss Perkins to see me trying to sew, but you can see. Take off your coat. Is it cold out?"

"Getting cold." The heavy coat was laid on one chair, and Carmencita, taking up a half-made gingham dress from another, sat in it and laid the garment in her lap. "I didn't know you knew how to sew."

"I don't." The girl at the machine laughed. "Those Simcoe children didn't have a dress to change in, and I'm practising on some skirts and waists for them. Every day I'm finding out something else I don't know how to do. I seem to have been taught a good many things there is no special need of knowing, and very few I can make use of down here."

"You didn't expect to come down here when you were learning

things, did you?" Carmencita's eyes were gravely watching the efforts being made to thread the machine's needle. "I guess when you were a little girl you didn't know there were things like you see down here. What made you come here, Miss Frances? You didn't have to. What made you come?"

Into the fine fair face color crept slowly, and for a moment a sudden frown ridged the high forehead from which the dark hair, parted and brushed back, waved into a loose knot at the back of her head; then she laughed, and her dark eyes looked into Carmencita's blue ones.

"Why did I come?" The gingham dress on which she had been sewing was folded carefully. "I came to find out some of the things I did not know about. I wasn't of any particular use to anybody else. No one needed me. I had a life on my hands that I didn't know what to do with, and I thought perhaps -"

"You could use it down here? You could use a dozen down here, but you weren't meant not to get married. Aren't you ever going to get married, Miss Frances?"

"I hardly think I will." Frances Barbour got up and pushed the machine against the wall. "The trouble about getting married is marrying the right man. One so often doesn't. I wouldn't like to make a mistake." Again she smiled.

"Don't see how you could make a mistake. Isn't there some way you can tell?"

"My dear Carmencita!" Stooping, the child's face was lifted and kissed. "I'm not a bit interested in men or marriage. They belong to - to a long, long time ago. I'm interested now in little girls like you, and in boys, and babies, and gingham dresses, and Christmas trees, and night classes, and the Dramatic School for the children who work, and -"

"I'm interested in them, too, but I'm going to get married when I'm big enough. I know you work awful hard down here, but it wasn't what you were born for. I'm always feeling, right inside me, right here" - Carmencita's hand was laid on her breast - "that you aren't going to stay here long, and it makes an awful sink sometimes. You'll go away and forget us, and get married, and go to balls and parties and wear satin slippers with buckles on them, and dance, and I'd do it, too, if I were you. Only - only I wish sometimes you hadn't come. It will be so much harder when you go away."

"But I'm not going away." At the little white bureau in the plainly furnished room of Mother McNeil's "Home," Frances stuck the pins brought from the machine into the little cushion and nodded gaily to the child now standing by her side. "I've tried the parties and balls and - all the other things, and for a while they were very nice; and then one day I found I was spending all my time getting ready for them and resting from them, and there was never time for anything else. If I had died it would not have mattered the least bit that I had lived. And -"

"Didn't you have a sweetheart that it mattered to? Not even one?"

Into hers Carmencita's eyes were looking firmly, and, turning from them, Frances made effort to laugh; then her face whitened.

"One can never be sure how much things matter to others, Carmencita. We can only be sure of how much they matter - to us. But it was Christmas we were to talk about. It's much nicer to talk about Christmas. We can't talk very long, for I meet the 'Little Mothers' at half past six, and after that I -"

"And I've got to go at half past five to meet Father when he's through with that wedding up-town, and then we're going shopping. I've got a lot to talk about. The Beckwith babies are awful sick. I guess it would be a good thing if they were to die. They are always having colic and cramps and croup, and they've got a coughing mother and a lazy father; but they won't die. Some babies never will. Did you know Mr. Rheinhimer had been on another spree?" Carmencita, feet fastened in the rounds of her chair, elbows on knees, and chin in the palms of her hand, nodded affirmatively at the face in front of her. "Worst one yet. He smashed all the window-panes in the bedroom, and broke two legs of their best chairs doing it, and threw the basin and pitcher out of the window. He says he'd give any man living five hundred dollars, if he had it, if he'd live with his wife a month and not shake her. She is awful aggravating. She's always in curl papers, and don't wear corsets, and nags him to death. She says she wishes you'd send him to a cure or something. And I want to tell you about Father's present."

For twenty minutes they talked long and earnestly. Carmencita's list of names and number of pennies were gone over again and again, and when at last she got up to go the perplexities of indecision and adjustment were mainly removed, and she sighed with satisfaction.

"I'm very much obliged to you for helping me fix it." The piece of paper was carefully pinned to the inside of the coat. "I'm not going to get anything but Father's present to-night. I won't have to go to school to-morrow, and I want the buying to last as long as possible. Isn't it funny the way Christmas makes you feel?"

Carmencita's hands came suddenly together, and, pressing them on her breast, her eyes grew big and shining. Standing first on one foot and then on the other, she swayed slightly forward, then gave a leap in the air.

"I can't help it, Miss Frances, I really can't! It's something inside me - something that makes me wish I was all the world's mother! And I'm so squirmy and thrilly and shivery, thinking of the things I'd do if I could, that sometimes I'm bound to jump - just bound to! I'm almost sure something nice is going to happen. Did you ever feel that way, Miss Frances?"

"I used to feel that way." The clear dark eyes for a moment turned from the eager ones of the child. "It's a very nice way to feel. When one is young - though perhaps it is not so much youth as hope in the heart, and love, and -"

"I don't love everybody. I loathe Miss Cattie Burns. She's the very old dev - I promised Father I wouldn't say even a true mean thing about anybody for a month, and I've done it twice! I'd much rather love people, though. I love to love! It makes you feel so nice and warm and homey. If I had a house I'd have everybody I know - I mean all the nice everybodies - to spend Christmas with me. Isn't it funny that at Christmas something in you gets so lonely for - for - I don't know what for, exactly, but it's something you don't mind so much not having at other times."

Carmencita's arms opened to their full length, then circled slowly, and her hands crossed around her neck. "It's the time to wipe out and forget things, Father says. It's the home-time and the heart-time and -" In her voice was sudden anxiety. "You are not going away for Christmas are you, Miss Frances?"

"Not for Christmas eve." She hesitated. "I'm not quite sure what I'm going to do on Christmas day. My people live in different places and far apart. It is all very different from what it used to be. When one is alone -"

She stopped abruptly and, going over to the window, looked down on the street below; and Carmencita, watching, saw the face turned from hers twist in sudden pain. For a moment she stood puzzled and helpless. Something she did not understand was troubling, something in which she could not help. What was it?

"You couldn't be alone at Christmas, Miss Frances." Slowly she came toward the window, and shyly her hand slipped into that of her friend. "There are too many wanting you. Father and I can't give fine presents or have a fine dinner, but there wouldn't be words in which to tell you how thankful we'd be if you'd spend it with us. Would you - would you come to us, Miss Frances?"

Into the eager blue eyes looking up the dark eyes looked down, and, looking, grew misty. "Dear child, I'd come to you if I were here, but I do not think I'll be here." Her head went up as if impatient with herself. "I'm going away on Christmas day - going -" She took out her watch hurriedly and looked at it. "It's after half past five, Carmencita. You will have to hurry or you won't see the wedding guests go in. Good-by, dear. Have a good time and tuck away all you see to tell me later. I will be so busy between now and Christmas, there will be no time for talking, but after Christmas - Why, you've got on your straw hat, Carmencita! Where is the winter one Miss Cattie gave you? She told me she had given you a perfectly good hat that would last a long time."

"She did." Carmencita's hands were stuck in the deep pockets of her long coat, and again her big blue eyes were raised to her friend's. "It would have lasted for ever if it hadn't got burned up. It fell in the fire and got burned up." Out in the hall she hesitated, then came back, opened the door, and put her head in. "It did get burned up, Miss Frances. I burned it. Good-by."

Late into the night Frances Barbour sat at her desk in the bare and poorly furnished room which she now called hers, and wrote letters, settled accounts, wrapped bundles, assorted packages, and made lists of matters to be attended to on the next day. When at last through, with the reaction that comes from overtired body and nerves she leaned back in her chair and let her hands fall idly in her lap, and with eyes that saw not looked across at the windows, on whose panes bits of hail were tapping weirdly. For some minutes thought was held in abeyance; then suddenly she crossed her arms on the table, and her face was hidden in them.

"Oh, Stephen! Stephen!" Under her breath the words came wearily. "We were so foolish, Stephen; such silly children to give each other up! All through the year I know, but never as I do at Christmas. And we - we are each other's, Stephen!" With a proud uplifting of her head she got up. "I am a child," she said, "a child who wants what it once refused to have. But until he understood -" Quickly she put out the light.

CHAPTER III

He was ashamed of himself for being ashamed. Why on earth should he hesitate to tell Peterkin he would dine alone on Christmas day? It was none of Peterkin's business how he dined, or where, or with whom. And still he had not brought himself to the point of informing Peterkin, by his order for dinner at home, that he was not leaving town for the holidays, that he was not invited to dine with any one else, and that there was no one he cared to invite to dine with him. It was the 22d of December, and the custodian in charge of his domestic arrangements had not yet been told what his plans were for the 25th. He had no plans.

He might go, of course, to one of his clubs. But worse than telling Peterkin that he would dine alone would be the public avowal of having nowhere to go which dining at the club would not only indicate, but affirm. Besides, at Christmas a club was ghastly, and the few who dropped in had a half-shamed air at being there and got out as quickly as possible. He could go to Hallsboro, but Hallsboro no longer bore even a semblance to the little town in which he had been born - had, indeed, become something of a big city, bustling, busy, and new, and offensively up-to-date; and nowhere else did he feel so much a stranger as in the place he had once called home. He was but twelve when his parents moved away, and eight months later died within a week of each other, and for years he had not been back. Had there been brothers and sisters - Well, there were no brothers and sisters, and by this time he should be used to the fact that he was very much alone in the world.

KATE LANGLEY BOSHER

Hands in his pockets, Stephen Van Landing leaned back in his chair and looked across the room at a picture on the wall. He did not see the picture; he saw, instead, certain things that were not pleasant to see. No, he would not go to Hallsboro for Christmas.

Turning off the light in his office and closing the door with unnecessary energy, Van Landing walked down the hall to the elevator, then turned away and toward the steps. Reaching the street, he hesitated as to the car he should take, whether one up-town to his club or one across to his apartment, and as he waited he watched the hurrying crowd with eyes in which were baffled impatience and perplexity. It was incomprehensible, the shopping craze at this season of the year. He wished there was no such season. Save for his very young childhood there were few happy memories connected with it, but only of late, only during the past few years, had the recurrence awakened within him a sort of horror, its approach a sense of loneliness that was demoralizing, and its celebration an emptiness in life that chilled and depressed beyond all reason. Why was it that as it drew near a feeling of cowardice so possessed him that he wanted to go away, go anywhere and hide until it was over, go where he could not see what it meant to others? It was humanity's home-time, and he had no home. Why -

"An ass that brays is wiser than the man who asks what can't be answered," he said, under his breath. "For the love of Heaven, quit it! Why-ing in a man is as inexcusable as whining in a woman. There's my car - crowded, of course!"

For some minutes longer he waited for a car on which there was chance to get a foothold, then, buttoning his overcoat, put his hands in his pockets and began the walk to his club. The season had been mild so far, but a change was coming, and the two days left for Christmas shopping would doubtless be stormy ones. On the whole, it might be fortunate. There was a good deal of nonsense in this curious custom of once a year getting on a giving jag, which was about what Christmas had degenerated into, and if something could prevent the dementia that possessed many people at this season it should be welcomed. It had often puzzled him, the behavior of the human family at this so-called Christian holiday in which tired people were overworked, poor people bought what they couldn't afford, and the rich gave unneeded things to the rich and were given unwanted ones in return. The hands of all people - all places - had become outstretched. It wasn't the giving of money that mattered. But what did matter was the hugeness of the habit which was commercializing a custom whose origin was very far removed from the spirit of the day.

With a shrug of his shoulders he shoved his hands deeper down into his pockets. "Quit again," he said, half aloud. "What do you know of the spirit of the day?"

Not only of the spirit of the day did he know little, but of late with acute conviction it was dawning on him that he knew little of many other things. Certainly he was getting little out of life. For a while, after professional recognition had come to him, and with it financial reward, he had tested society, only to give it up and settle down to still harder work during the day and his books when the day was done. The only woman he had ever wanted to marry had refused to marry him. His teeth came down on his lips. He still wanted her. In all the world there was but one woman he loved or could love, and for three years he had not seen her. It was his fault. He was to blame. It had taken him long to see it, but he saw it now. There had been a difference of opinion, a frank revealing of opposing points of view, and he had been told that she would not surrender her life to the selfishness that takes no part in activities beyond the interests of her own home. He had insisted that when a woman marries said home and husband should alone claim her time and heart, and in the multitude of demands which go into the cultural and practical development of a home out of a house there would be sufficient opportunity for the exercise of a woman's brain and ability. He had been such a fool. What right had he to limit her, or she him? It had all been so silly and such a waste, such a horrible waste of happiness.

For she had loved him. She was not a woman to love lightly, as he was not a man, and hers was the love that glorifies life. And he had lost it. That is, he had lost her. Three years ago she had broken their engagement. Two years of this time had been spent abroad. A few months after their return her mother died and her home was given up. Much of the time since her mother's death had been spent with her married sisters, who lived in cities far separated from one another, but not for some weeks had he heard anything concerning her. He did not even know where she was, or where she would be Christmas.

"Hello, Van!"

The voice behind made him turn. The voice was Bleeker McVeigh's.

"Where are the wedding garments? Don't mean you're not going!"

"Going where?" Van Landing fell into step. "Whose wedding?"

McVeigh lighted a fresh cigarette. "You ought to be hung. I tell you now you won't be bidden to my wedding. Why did you tell Jockie you'd come, if you didn't intend to?"

Van Landing stopped and for a minute stared at the man beside him. "I forgot this was the twenty-second," he said. "Tell Jock I'm dead. I wish I were for a week."

"Ought to be dead." McVeigh threw his match away. "A man who ignores his fellow-beings as you've ignored yours of late has no right to live. Better look out. Don't take long to be forgotten. Good night."

It was true that it didn't take long to be forgotten. He had been finding that out rather dismally of late, finding out also that a good many things Frances had told him about himself were true. Her eyes could be so soft and lovely and appealing; they were wonderful eyes, but they could blaze as well. And she was right. He was selfish and conventional and intolerant. That is, he had been. He wished he could forget her eyes. In all ways possible to a man of his type he had tried to forget, but forgetting was beyond his power. Jock had loved half a dozen women and this afternoon he was to be married to his last love. Were he on Jock's order he might have married. He wasn't on Jock's order.

Reaching his club, he started to go up the steps, then turned and walked away. To go in would provoke inquiry as to why he was not at the wedding. He took out his watch. It was twenty minutes of the hour set for the ceremony. He had intended to go, but - Well, he had forgotten, and was glad of it. He loathed weddings.

As he reached the building in which was his apartment he again hesitated and again walked on. An unaccountable impulse led him in the direction of the house, a few blocks away, in which his friend was to be married, and as he neared it he crossed the street and in the darkness of the late afternoon looked with eyes, half mocking, half amazed, at the long line of limousines which stretched from one end of the block to the other. At the corner he stopped. For some minutes he stood looking at the little group of people who made effort to press closer to the entrance of the awning which stretched from door to curbing, then turned to go, when he felt a hand touch him lightly on the arm.

"If you will come up to the top of the steps you can see much better," he heard a voice say. "I've seen almost everybody go in. I just ran down to tell you."

CHAPTER IV

Turning, Van Landing looked into the little face upraised to his, then lifted his hat. She was so enveloped in the big coat which came to her heels that for half a moment he could not tell whether she was ten or twenty. Then he smiled.

"Thank you," he said. "I don't know that I care to see. I don't know why I stopped."

"Oh, but it is perfectly grand, seeing them is! You can see everything up there" - a little bare hand was waved behind her in the direction of the porch - "and nothing down here. And you looked like you wanted to see. There have been kings and queens, and princes and princesses, and dukes and duchesses, and sirs, and -" She looked up. "What's the lady name for sir? 'Tisn't siress, is it?"

"I believe not." Van Landing laughed. "I didn't know there was so much royalty in town." "There is. They are royals - that kind of people." Her hand pointed in the direction of the house from which could be heard faint strains of music. "They live in palaces, and wave wands, and eat out of gold plates, and wear silk stockings in the morning, and - oh, they do everything that's splendid and grand and magnificent and -"

"Do you think people are splendid and grand and magnificent because they live in palaces and wear -"

"Goodness gracious!" The big blue eyes surveyed the speaker

with uncertainty. "Are you one of them, too?"

"One what?"

"Damanarkists. Mr. Leimberg is one. He hates people who live in palaces and wave wands and have _dee_-licious things to eat. He don't believe in it. Mr. Ripple says it's because he's a damanarkist and very dangerous. Mr. Leimberg thinks men like Mr. Ripple ought to be tarred and feathered. He says he'd take the very last cent a person had and give it to blood-suckers like that" - and again the red little hand was waved toward the opposite side of the street. "Mr. Ripple collects our rent. I guess it does take a lot of money to live in a palace, but I'd live in one if I could, though I'd try not to be very particular about rents and things. And I'd have chicken-pie for dinner every day and hot oysters for supper every night; and I'd ask some little girls sometimes to come and see me - that is, I think I would. But maybe I wouldn't. It's right easy to forget in a palace, I guess. Oh, look - there's somebody else going in! Hurry, mister, or you won't see!"

Following the child up the flight of stone steps, Van Landing stood at the top and looked across at the arriving cars, whose occupants were immediately lost to sight in the tunnel, as his new acquaintance called it, and then he looked at her.

Very blue and big and wonder-filled were her eyes, and, tense in the effort to gain the last glimpse of the gorgeously gowned guests, she stood on tiptoe, leaning forward eagerly, and suddenly Van Landing picked her up and put her on top of the railing. Holding on to his coat, the child laughed gaily.

"Aren't we having a good time?" Her breath was drawn in joyously. "It's almost as good as being inside. Wouldn't you like to be? I would. I guess the bride is beautiful, with real diamonds on her slippers and in her hair, and -" She looked down on Van Landing. "My father is in there. He goes to 'most all the scrimptious weddings that have harps to them. He plays on the harp when the minister is saying the words.

Do you think it is going to be a very long wedding?"

A note of anxiety in the child's voice made Van Landing look at her more closely, and as she raised her eyes to his something stirred within him curiously. What an old little face it was! All glow and eagerness, but much too thin and not half enough color, and the hat over the loose brown curls was straw.

"I don't think it will be long." His voice was cheerfully decisive. "That kind is usually soon over. Most of a wedding's time is taken in getting ready for it. Did you say your father was over there?"

The child's head nodded. "They have a harp, so I know they are nice people. Father can't give lessons any more, because he can't see but just a teensy, weensy bit when the sun is shining. He used to play on a big organ, and we used to have oysters almost any time, but that was before Mother died. Father was awful sick after she died, and there wasn't any money, and when he got well he was almost blind, and he can't teach any more, and 'most all he does now is weddings and funerals. I love him to go to weddings. He makes the others tell him everything they see, and then he tells me, and we have the grandest time making out we were sure enough invited, and talking of what we thought was the best thing to eat, and whose dress was the prettiest, and which lady was the loveliest - Oh, my goodness! Look there!"

Already some of the guests were departing; and Van Landing, looking at his watch, saw it was twenty minutes past six. Obviously among those present were some who failed to feel the enthusiasm for weddings that his new friend felt. With a smile he put the watch away, and, placing the child's feet more firmly on the railing, held her so that she could rest against his shoulder. She could hardly be more than twelve or thirteen, and undersized for that, but the oval face was one of singular intelligence, and her eyes - her eyes were strangely like the only eyes on earth he had ever loved, and as she settled herself more comfortably his heart warmed curiously, warmed as it had not done for years. Presently she looked down at him.

"I don't think you're a damanarkist." Her voice was joyous. "You're so nice. Can you see good?"

"Very good. There isn't much to see. One might if it weren't for that -"

"Old tunnel! I don't think they ought to have them if it isn't snowing or raining. Oh, I do hope Father can come out soon! If I tell you something will you promise not to tell, not even say it to yourself out loud?" Her face was raised to his. "I'm going to get Father's Christmas present to-night. We're going down-town when he is through over there. He can't see me buy it, and it's something he wants dreadfully. I've been saving ever since last Christmas. It's going to cost two dollars and seventy-five cents." The eager voice trailed off into an awed whisper. "That's an awful lot to spend on something you're not bound to have, but Christmas isn't like any other time. I spend millions in my mind at Christmas. Have you bought all your things, Mr. - Mr. - don't even know your name." She laughed. "What's your name, Mr. Man?"

Van Landing hesitated. Caution and reserve were inherent characteristics. Before the child's eyes they faded.

"Van Landing," he said. "Stephen Van Landing."

"Mine is Carmencita. Father named me that because when I was a teensy baby I kicked my feet so, and loved my tambourine best of all my things. Have you bought all your Christmas gifts, Mr. Van - I don't remember the other part."

"I haven't any to buy - and no one to buy for. That is -"

"Good gracious!" The child turned quickly; in her eyes and voice incredulity was unrestrained. "I didn't know there was anybody in all the world who didn't have anybody to buy for! Are you - are you very poor, Mr. Van? You look very nice."

KATE LANGLEY BOSHER

"I think I must be very poor." Van Landing fastened his glasses more securely on his nose. "I'm quite sure of it. It has been long since I cared to buy Christmas presents. I give a few, of course, but -"

"And don't you have Christmas dinner at home, and hang up your stocking, and buy toys and things for children, and hear the music in the churches? I know a lot of carols. Father taught me. I'll sing one for you. Want me? Oh, I believe they are coming out! Father said they wouldn't want him as long as the others. If I lived in a palace and was a royal lady I'd have a harp longer than anything else, but Father says it's on account of the food. Food is awful high, and people would rather eat than hear harps. Oh, there's Father! I must go, Mr. Van. Thank you ever so much for holding me."

With a movement that was scientific in its dexterity the child slipped from Van Landing's arms and jumped from the railing to the porch, and without so much as a turn of the head ran down the steps and across the street. Darting in between two large motor-cars, Van Landing saw her run forward and take the hand of a man who was standing near the side-entrance of the house in which the wedding had taken place. It was too dark to distinguish his face, and in the confusion following the calling of numbers and the hurrying off of guests he felt instinctively that the man shrank back, as is the way of the blind, and an impulse to go over and lead him away made him start down the steps.

At the foot he stopped. To go over was impossible. He would be recognized. For half a moment he hesitated. It was his dinner hour, and he should go home; but he didn't want to go home. The stillness and orderliness of his handsome apartment was suddenly irritating. It seemed a piece of mechanism made to go so smoothly and noiselessly that every element of humanness was lacking in it; and with something of a shiver he turned down the street and in the direction opposite to that wherein he lived. The child's eyes had stirred memories that must be kept down; and she was right. He was a poor man. He had a house, but no home, and he had no Christmas presents to buy.

CHAPTER V

"Mr. Van! Mr. Van!"

He turned quickly. Behind, his new-made acquaintance was making effort to run, but to run and still hold the hand of her father was difficult. With a smile he stopped.

"Oh, Mr. Van!" The words came breathlessly. "I was so afraid we would lose you! Father can't cross quick, and once I couldn't see you. Here he is, Father." She took Van Landing's hand and laid it in her father's. "He can tell by hands," she said, "whether you're a nice person or not. I told him you didn't have anybody, and -"

Van Landing's hand for a moment lay in the stranger's, then he shook the latter's warmly and again raised his hat. In the circle of light caused by the electric lamp near which they stood the blind man's face could be seen distinctly, and in it was that one sees but rarely in the faces of men, and in Van Landing's throat came sudden tightening.

"Oh, sir, I cannot make her understand, cannot keep her from talking to strangers!" The troubled voice was of a strange quality for so shabbily clothed a body, and in the eyes that saw not, and which were lifted to Van Landing's, was sudden terror. "She believes all people to be her friends. I cannot always be with her, and some day -"

"But, Father, you said that whoever didn't have any friends

must be our friend, because - because that's all we can be - just friends. And he hasn't any. I mean anybody to make Christmas for. He said so himself. And can't he go with us to-night and see the shops? I know he's nice, Father. Please, please let him!"

The look of terrified helplessness which for a moment swept over the gentle face, wherein suffering and sorrow had made deep impress, but in which was neither bitterness nor complaint, stirred the heart within him as not for long it had been stirred, and quickly Van Landing spoke.

"It may not be a good plan generally, but this time it was all right," he said. "She spoke to me because she thought I could not see what was going on across the street, and very kindly shared her better position with me. I -" He hesitated. His name would mean nothing to the man before him. Their worlds were very different worlds. It was possible, however, that this gentle, shrinking creature, with a face so spiritualized by life's denials that it shamed him as he looked, knew more of his, Van Landing's, world than he of the blind man's, and suddenly, as if something outside himself directed, he yielded to a strange impulse.

It was true, what the child had said. He had few friends - that is, friends in the sense the child meant. Of acquaintances he had many, very many. At his club, in business, in a rather limited social set, he knew a number of people well, but friends - If he were to die to-morrow his going would occasion but the usual comment he had often heard concerning others. Some years ago he had found himself continually entertaining what he called his friends, spending foolish sums of money on costly dinners, and quite suddenly he had quit. As long as he entertained he was entertained in return, and for some time after he stopped he still received invitations of many sorts, but in cynical realization of the unsatisfactoriness of his manner of life he had given it up, and in its place had come nothing to answer the hunger of his heart for comradeship and human cheer. His opinion of life had become unhealthy. As an experience for which one is not primarily responsible it had to be endured, but out of it he had gotten little save what men called success; and that, he had long since found, though sweet in the pursuit, was bitter in achievement if there was no one who cared - and for his nobody really cared. This blind man with the shabby clothes and ill-nourished body was richer than he. He had a child who loved him and whom he loved.

"It is true what your little girl has told you." Van Landing took off his glasses and wiped them. "I have no one to make Christmas for, and if you don't mind I wish you would let me go with you to the shops to-night. I don't know much about Christmas buying. My presents are chiefly given in mon - I mean I don't know any little children."

"And I know forty billion!" Carmencita's arms were out-stretched and her hands came together with ecstatic emphasis. "If I didn't stop to blink my eyes between now and Christmas morning I couldn't buy fast enough to fill all the stockings of the legs I know if I had the money to buy with. There's Mrs. McTarrens's four, and the six Blickers, and the ashman's eight, and the Roysters, and little Sallie Simcoe, and old Mr. Jenkinson, and Miss Becky who mends pants and hasn't any front teeth, and Mr. Leimberg. I'd get him specs. He has to hold his book like this" - and the palms of two little red hands were held close to Carmencita's eyes. "Oh, Father, please let him go!"

Hesitating, the blind man's eyes were again upturned, and again Van Landing spoke.

"You are right to be careful; but you need not fear. My name is Van Landing, and my office -"

"You are a gentleman!" Two hands with their long slender fingers were outstretched, and swiftly they stroked Van Landing's arms and body and face. "Your voice, your hands, tell me your class, and your clothes that you have money. Why - oh, why do you want to go with us?" Quickly his right hand drew his child toward him, and in terror he pressed her to his side. "She is my all, my light, my life! Away from her I am in darkness you could not understand. No, you must not go with us. You must go away and leave us!"

For a moment Van Landing hesitated, puzzled by the sudden fear in the man's face, then over his own crept grayness, and the muscles in it stiffened.

"My God!" he said, and his mouth grew dry. "Have men brought men to this?"

For another half-moment there was silence which the child, looking from one to the other, could not understand, and her hands, pressed close to her breast, gripped tightly her cold fingers. Presently Van Landing turned.

"Very well," he said. "I will go. It was just that I know little of a real Christmas. Good night."

"Oh, don't go - don't go, Mr. Van! It's going to be Christmas two days after to-morrow, Father, and the Christ-child wouldn't like it if you let him go!" Carmencita held the sleeve of Van Landing's coat with a sturdy clutch. "He isn't a damanarkist. I can tell by his eyes. They are so lonely-looking. You aren't telling a story, are you Mr. Van? Is it truly truth that you haven't anybody?"

"It is truly truth," he said. "I mean anybody to make Christmas for."

"No mother or father or a little girl like me? Haven't you even got a wife?"

"Not even a wife." Van Landing smiled.

"You are as bad as Miss Barbour. She hasn't anybody, either, now, she says, 'most everybody being -"

"Miss who?" Van Landing turned so sharply that the child jumped. "Who did you say?"

"Miss Barbour." The eyes which were so like those he could not forget were raised to his. "If you knew Miss Barbour she could tell you of plenty of people to make Christmas for. She's living right now with Mother McNeil, who isn't really anybody's mother, but just everybody's. But she don't live there all the time. Most of her people are dead or married and don't need her, so she came to Mother McNeil to see how children down there live. What's the matter, Mr. Van?"

To hide the upleaping flame in his face and the sudden trembling of his hands Van Landing stooped down and picked up the handkerchief he had dropped; then he stepped back and out of the circle of light in which he had been standing. For a moment he did not speak lest his voice be as unsteady as his hands, but, taking out his watch, he looked at it, then put it back with fumbling fingers.

"Her first name - Miss Barbour's first name," he said, and the dryness of his throat made his words a little indistinct. "What is it?"

With mouth rounded into a little ball, Carmencita blew on her stiff finger-tips. "Frances," she said, and first one foot and then the other was stamped for purpose of warmth. "The damanarkist says God made her, but the devil has more to do with most women than anybody else. He don't like women. Do you know her, Mr. Van?"

"If your friend is my friend - I know her very well," he said, and put his hands in his pockets to hide the twitching of his fingers. "A long time ago she was the only real friend I had, and I lost her. I have wanted very much to find her."

"Oh, Father, if he knows Miss Barbour he's bound to be all right!" Carmencita's arms were flung above her head and down again, and on her tiptoes she danced gaily round and round.

"We can show him where she lives." She stopped. "No, we can't. She told me I must never do that. I mustn't send any one to her, but I could tell her of anybody I wanted her to know about." Head uplifted, her eyes searched Van Landing's, and her words came in an awed whisper, "Was - was she your sweetheart, Mr. Van?"

"She was." Again Van Landing wiped his forehead. It didn't in the least matter that he was telling to this unknown child the most personal of matters. Nothing mattered but that perhaps he might find Frances. "You must take me to her," he said. "I must see her to-night."

"I can't take you to see her to-night. She wouldn't like it. Oh, I know!" Carmencita made another rapid whirl. "We can go down-town and get" - she nodded confidentially to her new-made friend and pointed her finger in her father's direction - "and then we can come back and have some toast and tea; and then I'll send for Miss Barbour to come quick, as I need her awful, and when she comes in you can say: 'Oh, my lost and loved one, here I am! We will be married right away, this minute!' I read that in a book once. Won't it be grand? But you won't -" The dancing ceased, and her hands stiffened in sudden anxiety. "You won't take her away, will you?"

"If she will come with me I will not take her where she won't come back. Can't we start?"

But the child was obdurate. She would do nothing until her purchase was made, and to her entreaties her father finally yielded, and a few minutes later Van Landing and his new acquaintances were on a down-town car, bound for a shopping district as unknown to him as the shops in which he was accustomed to deal were unknown to them.

Still a bit dazed by his chance discovery, he made no comment on the child's continual chatter, but let her exuberance and delight have full play while he tried to adjust himself to a realization that made all thought but a chaotic mixture of hope and doubt, of turbulent fear and determined purpose, and of one thing only was he sure. Three years of his life had been wasted. Another hour should not be lost were it in his power to prevent.

CHAPTER VI

When the store was reached Van Landing for the first time was able to see distinctly the faces of Carmencita and her father, and as for a moment he watched the slim little body in its long coat, once the property, undoubtedly, of a much bigger person, saw her eager, wonder-filled eyes, and the wistful mouth which had learned to smile at surrender, the strings of his heart twisted in protest, and for the "damanarkist" of whom she had spoken, for the moment he had sympathy of which on yesterday there would have been no understanding. She could not be more than twelve or thirteen, he thought, but condition and circumstance had made her a woman in many matters, and the art of shopping she knew well. Slowly, very slowly, she made her way to the particular counter at which her precious purchase was to be made, lingering here and there to gaze at things as much beyond her hope of possession as the stars of heaven; and, following her slow-walking, Van Landing could see her eyes brighten and yearn, her lips move, her hand outstretch to touch and then draw back quickly, and also every now and then he could see her shake her head.

"What is it?" he asked. "Why do you do that? Is there anything in here you would like to get, besides the thing you came for?"

"Anything I'd like to get!" The words were repeated as if not heard aright. "Anybody would know you'd never been a girl. There isn't much in here I wouldn't like to get if I didn't have to pay for it."

KATE LANGLEY BOSHER

"But not rattles and dolls and drums and pop-guns and boxing-gloves and all the other things you've looked at. Girls of your age -"

"This girl wasn't looking at them for herself. I'm 'most grown up now. But everybody on our street has got a baby, and a lot of children besides. Mrs. Perry has twins and a baby, and Mrs. Latimer always has two on a bottle at the same time. I'm just buying things in my mind. It's the only way I can buy 'em, and Christmas wouldn't be Christmas if you couldn't buy some way. Sallie Simcoe will go crazy if she don't get a doll that whistles. She saw one in a window once. It was a Whistling Jim and cost a dollar. She won't get it. Oh, here it is, Mr. Van! Here's the counter where the jewelry things are."

As she neared it she nodded to Van Landing and pointed to her father, who, hand on her shoulder, had kept close to her, then beckoned him to come nearer. "He can't see, I know" - her voice was excited - "but take him away, won't you? I wouldn't have him guess it, not for *anything* on earth! I'll be through in a minute."

In moments incredibly few, but to Van Landing tormentingly long, she was back again, and close to her heart she was hugging a tiny package with one hand, while the other was laid on her father's arm. "I got it," she whispered; "it's perfectly beautiful." She spoke louder. "I guess we'd better be going now. I know you're hungry, and so am I. Come on. We can walk home, and then I'll make the tea."

For a second Van Landing hesitated, then he followed the odd-looking couple out into the street, but as they started to turn the corner he stopped.

"I say" - he cleared his throat to hide its embarrassed hesitation - "don't you want to do me a favor? Where I live I don't buy the things I eat, and I've often thought I'd like to. If you are going to make the tea and toast, why can't I get the - the chicken, say, and some salad and things? That's a good-looking window over there with cooked stuff in it. We'll have a party and each put in something."

"Chicken?" Into his face the child gazed with pitying comprehension of his ignorance, and in her voice was shrill amusement. "*Chicken!* Did you ever price one? I have, when I'm having kings and queens taking dinner with me in my mind. People don't have chicken 'cept at Christmas, and sometimes Sundays if there hasn't been anybody out of work for a long time. Come on. I've got a box of sardines. Just think, Father, he wants to buy a *chicken!*"

With a gay little laugh in which was shrewd knowledge of the unthinkableness of certain indulgences, the child slipped one arm through her father's and another through Van Landing's, and with a happy skip led the way down the poorly lighted street. A solid mass of dreary-looking houses, with fronts unrelieved by a distinguishing feature, stretched as far as the eye could see, and when a few blocks had been walked it was with a sense of relief that a corner was turned and Van Landing found himself at the foot of a flight of steps up which the child bounded and beckoned him to follow.

The house was like the others, one of a long row, and dull and dark and dingy, but from its basement came a baby's wailing, while from the floor above, as the hall was entered, could be heard the rapid click of a sewing-machine. Four flights of steps were mounted; then Carmencita took the key from her father's pocket and opened the door.

"This is our suite," she said, and courtesied low. "Please strike a match, if you have one, Mr. Van. This house is very old, and history houses don't have electric lights. The ghosts wouldn't like it. Some of my best friends are ghosts. I'll be back in a minute."

As she ran into the little hall room adjoining the large room which he saw comprised their "suite," Van Landing lighted the lamp near the mantel and looked around. In the center was a marble-topped table, and on it a lamp, a work-basket, and several magazines with backs half gone. The floor was bare save for a small and worn rug here and there, and on the sills of the uncurtained windows two hardy geraniums were blooming bravely. A chest of drawers, a few chairs, a shelf of books, a rug-covered cot, a corner cupboard, a wash-stand behind a screen, and a small table near the stove, behind which a box of wood could be seen, completed its furnishings; and still, despite its bareness, there was something in it which was not in the place wherein he lived, and wonderingly he again looked around. Had he found himself in the moon or at the bottom of the Dead Sea it would be hardly less remarkable than finding himself here. Adventures of this sort were entirely out of his experience. As regulated as a piece of machinery his life had become of late, and the routine of office and club and house had been accepted as beyond escape, and the chance meeting of this little creature -

"Oh, my goodness! I forgot to put the kettle on!"

With a spring that came apparently from the door opposite the stove near which he was standing Carmencita was by his side, and, swift movement following swift movement, the lid of the stove was lifted, wood put in, the kettle of water put on, and the table drawn farther out in the floor. A moment more the lamp was lighted, her father's coat and hat in place, his chair drawn up to the now roaring fire; then, with speculation in her eyes, she stood for half a moment, hands on hips, looking first at Van Landing and then at the cupboard in the corner.

For the first time he saw well the slender little body out of its long, loose coat, the heavy, brown curls which tumbled over the oval face, the clear eyes that little escaped, so keen was their quality, and the thin legs with their small feet in large shoes, and as he looked he smiled.

"Well," he asked, "can I help you? You seem very uncertain."

"I am. Put your hat and coat over there" - she pointed to the covered cot close to the wall - "then come back and tell me."

He did as directed and, hands in pockets, stood again in front of her. "Is" - his face whitened - "is it about Miss Barbour? Can you send her word?"

"Send now? I guess not!" On tiptoes the child looked for something on the mantel-piece. "We haven't had supper yet, and I'm so hungry I could eat air. Besides, she has a class to-night - The Little Big Sisters. I'm one when I can go, but I can't go often." She waved her hand in the direction of her father. "I'll send for her 'bout half past nine. Which do you like best, sardines with lemon on 'em, or toasted cheese on toast with syrup afterward? Which?"

The tone was one of momentous inquiry. Miss Barbour's coming was a matter that could wait, but supper necessitated a solemn decision which must be made at once. Hands clasped behind her, the blue eyes grew big with suspense, and again she repeated, "Which?"

"I really don't know. Both are very good. I believe I like sardines better than - Oh no, I don't." He had caught the flicker of disappointment in the anxious little face. "I mean I think toasted cheese the best thing to eat that's going. Let's have that!"

"All right." With another spring the child was at the cupboard, and swiftly she went to work. "Read to father, won't you?" she called, without looking round. "In that magazine with the geranium leaf sticking out is where I left off. You'll have to read right loud."

Drawing his chair close to the lighted lamp, Van Landing took his seat near the blind musician, and for the first time noticed the slender, finely formed fingers of the hands now resting on the arms of the chair in which he sat; noticed the shiny, well-worn coat and the lock of white hair that fell across the high forehead; saw the sensitive mouth; and as he looked he wondered as to the story that was his. An old one, perhaps. Born of better blood than his present position implied, he had evidently found the battle of life more than he was equal to, and, unfit to fight, he had doubtless slipped down and down in the scale of human society until to-day he and his child were dwellers on the borderland of the slums.

He found the article and began to read. The technicalities of musical composition had never appealed to him, but, though by him the writer's exhaustive knowledge of his subject was not appreciated, by his listener it was greatly so, and, in tense eagerness to miss no word, the latter leaned forward and kept his sightless eyes in the direction of the sound of his voice.

Not for long could he read, however. In a few moments Carmencita's hands were outstretched, and, giving one to each, she led them to the table, and at it he sat down as naturally as though it were a familiar occurrence. In the center was a glass jar with a spray of red geranium in it, and behind the earthen tea-pot the child presided with the ease of long usage. As she gave him his tea he noticed it was in the only unchipped cup, and on the one kept for herself there was no handle. Under his breath he swore softly. Why - He mentally shook himself. This was no time for why-ing.

As an appetizer the toasted cheese on toasted bread was excellent, but the supper - if she had only let him get it. He had not dared insist, and never had he been more consciously a guest, but could people live on fare so scant as this? It was like Frances to want to know how other people lived - and not to be content with knowing. But after she knew how could she sleep at night? Great God! If there was to be a day of judgment what could men say - men like himself and his friends?

CHAPTER VII

For half an hour longer Carmencita chatted gaily, offering dish after dish of imaginary food with the assurance that it would cause no sickness or discomfort, and at the child's spirit and imagination Van Landing marveled. The years of ignorance and indifference, in which he had not cared to know what Frances knew all men should know, came back disquietingly, and he wondered if for him it were too late.

As Carmencita got up to clear the table he took out his watch and looked at it, then put it quickly back lest she should see. Who was going to take the note? Why couldn't he go to the place at which was held the class of Little Big Sisters and get Frances? With a quick indrawing breath he handed his host cigars.

"I hope you smoke," he said; "that is, if Carmencita does not object."

"Oh, I don't object. Smoke!" Carmencita's hand was waved. "After I wash the dishes I'll write the note, then I'll go down and get Noodles to take it. I'll ask Mr. Robinsky to bring the harp up, Father. He brought it home for us; he's a flute-er." The explanation was made to Van Landing. "He always brings it home when Father and I are going somewhere else. Smoke, please. I love to smell smoke smell."

With a splash the remaining water in the tea-kettle was poured in the dish-pan, and for a few moments the clatter of knives

KATE LANGLEY BOSHER

and forks and spoons prevented talk. Over the blind man's face crept the content that comes from a good cigar, and in silence he and his guest smoked while Carmencita did her work. Not long was there silence, however, for very shortly the child was on a stool at Van Landing's feet, in her hands a pad of paper, and on her knee a backless magazine.

For half a minute she looked in Van Landing's face. "Isn't it nice and funny - your being here? I like you." Her voice was joyous. "If I tell you something, you won't tell?" She leaned forward, hands on his knees. "This afternoon before I went out I asked God please to let something nice happen. There hasn't anything very nice happened for so long, I was afraid He had forgot. What must I write, Mr. Van?"

Into Van Landing's face the color surged, then died away and left it strangely white. The child's eyes were holding his, and he did not try to avoid them. It didn't matter. The only thing that mattered was to get Frances quickly.

"Tell her I must see her to-night, that I must come to her. Why can't I go to her, Carmencita?"

"Because she doesn't want anybody to come to see her that she doesn't tell to come. She told me so herself, and I wouldn't break her rules for a gold ring with a ruby in it. I know. I'll tell her I'm bound to show her something to-night or I won't sleep a wink. And you'll be *It!* You can go in Father's room, and when she comes in you will come out and say - What will you say, Mr. Van?"

"I don't know. Perhaps I sha'n't say anything. Sometimes one can't."

"I'll look in that book I read once and see what he said, if you want me to. It was a beautiful book. It had an awful lot of love in it. I know what I'm going to write."

For some moments she wrote laboriously on the pad, which

wabbled badly on her knees, then she folded the piece of paper and, getting up, went toward the door. Van Landing followed her.

"The boy," he said. "Will you give him this and tell him if the note is delivered to Miss Barbour personally there will be more when he comes back?" He held out his hand.

As if not seeing aright, Carmencita looked closely at what was held toward her, then up in Van Landing's face. "You must have plenty of money, if you haven't any friends," she said, and in her voice was faint suspicion. "Noodles can't have that. He'd never go anywhere for me again if he got that much." Her hand waved his away. "When he comes back, if you'll give him a quarter he'll stand on his head. It's hard and hollow, and he makes right smart standing on it and wriggling his feet." She shook her head. "It would ruin him to give him a dollar. Please read to Father."

Her visitor's face flushed. Why couldn't he remember? "Very well," he said; "manage it your way. Tell him to hurry, will you?'"

Would she come? With his lips Stephen Van Landing was pronouncing the words of the article he had again begun to read to the blind harpist, but in his heart, which was beating thickly, other words were surging, and every now and then he wiped his forehead lest its dampness be seen by the child's keen eyes. Would she come? Three years had passed since senseless selfishness on his part had made her spirit flare and she had given him back his ring. For a moment he had held it, and in the dancing flames of the logs upon the hearth in the library of her beautiful old-fashioned home its stones had gleamed brilliantly, flashed protesting fire; then he had dropped it in the blaze and turned and left the room. Had she forgotten, or had she suffered, too?

With mechanical monotony the words continued to come from his lips, but his thoughts were afar off, and presently

Carmencita took the magazine out of his hand.

"Excuse me," she said, "but Father is asleep, and you don't know a word you're saying. You might as well stop."

Putting the magazine on the table, Carmencita drew the stool on which she was sitting closer to Van Landing's chair, and, hands clasped around her knees, looked up into his eyes. In hers was puzzled questioning.

"I beg your pardon." His face flushed under the grave scrutiny bent upon him. "I was reading abominably, but I couldn't get my mind -"

"I know," Carmencita nodded understandingly. "I do that way sometimes when I'm saying one thing and thinking another, and Father always takes a little nap until I get out of the clouds. He says I spend a lot of my time in the clouds. I'm bound to soar sometimes. If I didn't make out I wasn't really and truly living here, on the top floor, with the Rheinhimers underneath, but just waiting for our house to be fixed up, I couldn't stand it all the time. I'd go -"

She hesitated, then again went on. "You see, it's this way. There 're a lot of things I hate, but I've got to stand them, and the only way I can do it is to get away from them in my mind sometimes. Father says it's the way we stand things that proves the kind of person we are; but Father is Father, and I am me, and letting out is a great relief. Did you ever feel as if you're bound to say things sometimes?"

"I'm afraid I've not only felt I had to say them, but I said them." Van Landing looked at his watch. "Your Father is doubtless right, but -"

"Noodles hasn't had time to get back yet, and she might not be there." Carmencita glanced toward the clock. "And Father is always right. He's had to sit so many hours alone and think and think and think, that he's had time to ask God about a good many things we don't take time to ask about. I pray a lot, but my kind of prayers isn't praying. They're mostly asking, and Father says prayer is receiving - is getting God in you, I mean. I don't understand, but he does, and he doesn't ask for things like I do, but for patience and courage and - and things like that. No matter what happens, he keeps on trusting. I don't. I'm not much of a truster. I want to do things my way, myself." She leaned forward. "If I tell you something will you promise not to tell anybody, not even Miss Frances when - when it's all right?"

"I promise."

Van Landing nodded at the eager little face upraised to his. It was singularly attractive and appealing, and the varying emotions that swept over it indicated a temperament that took little in life calmly, or as a commonplace happening, and a surge of protest at her surroundings swept over him.

"I promise," he repeated. "I won't tell."

"Cross your heart and shut your eyes and I will tell you."

Hands on his knees, Carmencita watched the awkward movements of Van Landing's fingers, then she laughed joyously, but when she spoke her voice was in a whisper.

"I'm writing a book."

"You are doing what?"

"Writing a book! It's perfectly grand. That is, some days it is, but most days it is a mess. It was a mess yesterday, and I burned up every single word I wrote last week. I'll show it to you if you want to see it."

Without waiting for an answer Carmencita sprang to her feet, and with noiseless movement skipped across the room, and from the middle drawer of the chest between the windows took out a large flat box.

"This is it." Again taking her seat on the stool at Van Landing's feet, she opened the box carefully. One by one she lifted out of it pieces of paper of varying size and color and held them toward her visitor, who, hands clasped between knees, was bending forward and watching with amazed interest the seemingly exhaustless contents of the box beside him.

"I use pad-paper when I have it." Several white sheets were laid in a pile by themselves. "But most of the chapters are on wrapping-paper. Mrs. Beckwith gives me all of hers, and so does Mrs. Rheinhimer when her children don't chew it up before she can save it. That's chapter fourteen. I don't like it much, it's so squshy, but I wrote it that way because I read in a newspaper once that slops sold better than anything else, and I'm writing this to sell, if I can."

"Have you named it?" Van Landing's voice was as serious as Carmencita's. "I've been told that a good title is a great help to a book. I hope yours will bring you a good deal of money, but -"

"So do I." Carmencita's hands came together fervently. "I'm bound to make some money, and this is the only way I can think of until I'm fourteen and can go to work. I'm just thirteen and two months, and I can't go yet. The law won't let me. I used to think it took a lot of sense to write a book, but the Damanarkist says it don't, and that anybody who is fool enough to waste time could write the truck people read nowadays. He don't read it, but I do, all I can get - I like it."

"I've never tried to write." Van Landing again glanced at the clock. Noodles was staying an interminably long time. "Like you, I imagined it took some measure of ability -"

"Oh, but it don't. I mean it doesn't take any to write things like that." Carmencita's finger pointed to several backless magazines and a couple of paper-bound books on the table behind her. "I read once that people like to read things that make them laugh and cry and - and forget about the rent money, and tell all about love-dovies and villains and beautiful maidens, and my book's got some of all those kinds of things in it. It hasn't got any - What did you say you thought it took to write a book?"

"Ability - that is, a little of it."

"I guess that depends on the kind of book it is. I put something of everything I could think of in mine, but I didn't put any ability in. I didn't have any to put, and, besides, I wanted it to sell. That's the chapter I love best." A large piece of brown paper was waved in the air. "It's the one in which the Princess Patricia gets ready to die because she hears her sweetheart making love to some one else, and then she comes to her senses and makes him marry the other girl so they can live miserable ever after, and the Princess goes about doing good like Miss Frances. But I'm going to marry her to somebody before I'm through - I'm -"

"You believe in marriage, then." Van Landing smiled, and, stooping, picked up several sheets of paper evidently torn from a blank-book. "This must be the courtship chapter. It seems rather sentimental."

"It is. Regular mush slush. It's the kind of courting a man who isn't much does - that is, I guess it's the kind, but the Princess understands. She's been fooled once. Tell me" - Carmencita leaned forward and, arms again crossed on Van Landing's knees, looked anxiously in his face - "what does a man say when he's really and truly courting? I mean a nice man. When the Real one comes, the Right one - what will he say? I'm just about there, and I don't know how to go on."

"I wish I could tell you." Van Landing leaned back in his chair and, taking out his watch again, looked at it. "I shouldn't dare to try to write a novel, consequently -"

"I'll try anything while I'm waiting to go to work." Carmencita sat back dejectedly. "Is a book a novel because it has love in it?"

"It is generally supposed to be. When you are older you may write your love scenes with greater knowledge and -"

"No, I won't. I don't expect to have any love scenes when I get married. I've read a lot of that, and it don't last. All I want my husband to say is, 'Will you marry me, Carmencita?' and I will say, 'Yes,' and I hope we'll keep on liking each other. Some don't." Her face changed, and she sat upright, her hands pressed to her breast. "*This* is a novel - to - night is! We're living one, and you're the Prince and Miss Frances is the Princess, and I found you! Oh, my goodness! what is that?"

With a swift movement she was on her feet and at the door. Van Landing, too, rose quickly. Below could be heard loud voices, the moving of furniture, and the cries of frightened children, and cautiously Carmencita turned the knob and went into the hall.

"Old Beer-Barrel is drunk again." Tiptoeing to the banister, she leaned over it. "When he gets like this he's crazy as a loon, and some day he'll kill somebody. Goodness gracious! he's coming up here!"

Before Van Landing could reach her she was inside and at the wash-stand. Taking up the pitcher filled with water, she again ran into the hall, and as the cursing, stumbling man began to mount the stairs she leaned over the banister and poured the contents of the pitcher on his head. As if shot, the man stood still, face upturned, hair drenched, hands trembling, then he sat down on the steps.

Giving the pitcher to Van Landing, she told him to fill it and pointed to a faucet in the hall. "I don't think he'll need another; one is generally enough. I've seen him like this before. His wife won't throw water in his face, but I throw." She leaned farther over the railing. "If you'll be quiet and go back quick I won't put any more water on you; it's awful cold, but if you don't -"

Slowly, and as if dazed, the man on the steps got up, and as he disappeared Carmencita nodded to her visitor to go back to her Father, now standing by the table. Closing the door, she came toward him and pushed him again in his chair, smoothing lightly the snow-white hair and kissing the trembling fingers, then at his feet she took her seat.

"I'm so sorry he waked you. It was just old Beer-Barrel. He oughtn't to drink" - she raised her eyes to Van Landing's - "but a man who's got a wife like his is bound to do something, and sometimes I wish I could put the water on her instead of him."

CHAPTER VIII

For a moment Van Landing walked up and down the room, hands in his pockets and heart pounding in a way of which he was ashamed. Ordinarily the sight of a drunken man would have awakened little emotion save disgust, but the realization of the helplessness of the two people before him filled him with inward rage, and for some time he could not trust himself to speak. A sickening horror of this hideous side of life filled him with strange protest. Yesterday he had not known and had not cared that such things could be, and now -

On Carmencita's face was none of the alarm that had come into his. Her father, too, was getting over his fright. For this helpless old man and fair, frail child, whose wit and courage were equal to situations of which she had the right of childhood to be ignorant, the scene just witnessed had the familiarity of frequent repetition, but for him it was horribly new, and if the Damanarkist of whom Carmencita so often spoke should come in he would be glad to shake his hand.

A noise at the door made him start. They were coming. The boy and Frances. He dug his hands deeper in his pockets to hide their trembling, and his face went white.

But it was not Noodles. It was Mr. Robinsky, who had brought the harp, and, though he evidently intended to sit down and talk, with consummate skill and grace he was led into the hall by Carmencita and told good night with sweetness and decision. It was wonderfully managed. No man could have done it, and in his heart Van Landing thanked her; but before he could speak there was a loud pounding on the door, and both he and Carmencita started nervously toward it.

"It's Noodles. I know his knock." Carmencita's hands clasped tightly, and in her voice was eager trembling. "I'm so excited I can't breathe good! It's like being in a book. Go in the room over there quick, Mr. Van. Come in!"

With inward as well as outward rigidity Van Landing waited. To the movements of Carmencita's hand waving him away he paid no attention. In thick, heavy throbs his heart sent the blood to his face, then it receded, and for a moment the room was dark and he saw nothing. To the "come in" of Carmencita the door opened, and he looked in its direction. Noodles was alone.

"Where is she?" Carmencita's voice was high and shrill in excitement and dismay. "I told you to wait for her! You know I told you to wait for her!"

Cap in hand, Noodles looked first at Van Landing and then at the child. "Warn't no her to wait for," he said, presently. "She ain't there, and she didn't go to the class to-night. Miss James went for her. Some of her kin-folks is in town staying with some their kin-folks, and she is spending the night with 'em." The now soiled and crumpled note was held toward Carmencita. "She won't be back till day after to-morrow, what's Christmas eve, though she might come back to-morrow night, Fetch-It said. Warn't nobody there but Fetch-It - leastways warn't nobody else I seen."

Van Landing looked at Carmencita, then turned sharply and went over toward the window. A choking, stifling sensation made breathing difficult, and, the tension of the past few hours relaxed, he felt as one on the edge of a precipice from which at any moment he might topple over. It was too cold to open the window, but he must have air. Going to the couch, he took up his hat and coat, then came back and held out his hand.

"Give him this" - he nodded at Noodles, "and tell your father good night. And thank you, Carmencita, thank you for letting me come. To-morrow -" The room was getting black. "I will see you to-morrow."

A moment later he was out of the room and down the steps and on the street, and in the darkness he walked as one who feels something in his way he cannot see; and then he laughed, and the laugh was hard and bitter, and in it was a sound that was not good to hear.

The cold air stung his face, made breathing better, and after a while he looked up. For many blocks he had walked unheedingly, but, hearing a church-bell strike the hour, he took out his watch and glanced at it. To go home was impossible. Turning into a side-street, he walked rapidly in a direction that led he knew not whither, and for a while let the stinging sensation of disappointment and rebellion possess him without restraint. It was pretty cruel, this sudden shutting of the door of hope in his face. The discovery of Frances's presence in the city had brought again in full tumultuous surge the old love and longing, and the hours of waiting had been well-nigh unendurable. And now he would have to wait until day after to-morrow. He would go to-morrow night to this Mother Somebody. What was her name? He could remember nothing, was, indeed, as stupid as if he had been knocked in the head. Well, he had been. Where did this woman live? The child had refused to tell him. With a sudden stop he looked around. Where was he? He had walked miles in and out of streets as unknown to him as if part of a city he had never been in, and he had no idea where he was. A sudden fear gripped him. Where did Carmencita live? He had paid no attention to the streets they were on when she took him to the house she called home. He was full of other thought, but her address, of course, he would get before he left, and he had left without asking. What a fool he was! What a stupid fool! For half a moment he looked uncertainly up and down the street whose name he did not know. No policeman was in sight; no one was in sight except a woman on the opposite pavement, who was scurrying along with something under her shawl hugged close to her breast, and a young girl who was coming his way. Turning, he retraced his steps. He did not know in which direction to go. He only knew he must keep on. Perhaps he could find his way back to the place where Carmencita lived.

He did not find it. Through the night he walked street after street, trying to recall some building he had passed, but he had walked as blind men walk, and nothing had been noticed. To ask of people what they could not tell was useless. He did not know the name of the street he wanted to find, and, moreover, a curious shrinking kept him from inquiring. In the morning he would find it, but he did not want to make demands upon the usual sources for help until he had exhausted all other means of redeeming his folly in not learning Carmencita's full name and address before he left her. Was a man's whole life to be changed, to be made or unmade, by whimsical chance or by stupid blunder? In the gray dawn of a new day he reached his home and went to bed for a few hours' sleep.

When, later, he left his house to renew his search for Carmencita the weather had changed. It had begun to snow, and tiny particles of ice stung his face as he walked, and the people who passed shivered as they hurried by. On every street that offered chance of being the one he sought he went up and down its length, and not until he felt he was being noticed did he take into partial confidence a good-natured policeman who had nodded to him on his third passing. The man was kindly, but for hay-stack needles there was no time and he was directed to headquarters. To find a house, number unknown, on a street, name unknown, of a party, full name again unknown, was too much of a puzzle for busy times like these. Any other time than Christmas - He was turned from that an inquiry from a woman with a child in her arms might be answered.

"Any other time than Christmas!"

With a sense of demoralization it was dawning on him that he might not find her, or Carmencita, in time for Christmas, and he *must* find them. A great hunger for the day to be to him what it seemed to be to others possessed him feverishly, and with eyes that saw what they had never seen before he watched, as he walked, the faces of the people who passed, and in his heart crept childish longing to buy something for somebody, something that was wanted very much, as these people seemed to be doing. He had made out the checks he usually sent to certain institutions and certain parties at this season of the year for his head clerk to mail. By this time they had been received, but with them had gone no word of greeting or good will; his card alone had been inclosed. A few orders had been left at various stores, but with them went no Christmas spirit. He wondered how it would feel to buy a thing that could make one's face look as Carmencita's had looked when she made her purchase of the night before. It was a locket she had bought - a gold locket.

In a whispered confidence while in the car she had told him it was for her mother's picture. The picture used to be in her father's watch, but the watch had to be sold when he was sick, after her mother's death, and he had missed the touch of the picture so. She knew, for often she had seen him holding his watch in his hand, open at the back, where the picture lay, with his fingers on it, and sometimes he would kiss it when he thought she was out of the room. After the watch was sold the picture had been folded up in one of her mother's handkerchiefs, and her father kept it in the pocket of his coat; but once it had slipped out of the handkerchief, and once through a hole in the pocket, and they thought it was lost. Her father hadn't slept any that night. And now he could sleep with the locket around his neck. She would put it on a ribbon. Wasn't it grand? And Carmencita's hands had clasped ecstatically.

Up and down the streets he went, looking, looking, looking. The district in which he found himself was one of the poorest in the city, but the shops were crowded with buyers, and, though the goods for sale were cheap and common and of a quality that at other times would have repelled, to-day they interested. Carmencita might be among the shoppers. She had said she had a few things to get for some children - penny things - and she was possibly out, notwithstanding the snow which now was falling thick and fast.

Some time after his usual lunch-hour he remembered he must have something to eat; and, going into a dingy-looking restaurant, he sat down at a table, the only one which had a vacant seat at it, and ordered coffee and oysters. His table companion was a half-grown boy with chapped hands and a thin white face; but his eyes were clear and happy, and the piece of pie he was eating was being swallowed in huge hunks. It was his sole order, a piece of awful-looking pie. As the coffee and oysters were brought him Van Landing saw the boy look at them hungrily and then turn his eyes away.

"I beg your pardon." Van Landing, whose well-regulated life permitted of few impulses, turned to the boy. "I ordered these things" - he pointed to the steaming food - "and I don't want them. I want something else. Would you mind having them? It's a pity to throw them away."

The boy hesitated, uncertain what was meant, then he laughed. "It sure is," he said. "If you don't want them I'll help you out. I'm hollow as a hound what's been on a hunt. Good thing Christmas don't come but once a year. You can cut out lunch better'n anything else for a save-up, though. That girl over there" - he pointed his finger behind him - "ain't had nothing but a glass of milk for a month. She's got some kiddie brothers and sisters, and they're bound to have Christmas, she says. Rough day, ain't it?"

Van Landing gave another order. Had it not been for the gnawing restlessness, the growing fear, which filled him, the scene would have interested. A few days ago he would have seen only the sordid side of it, the crudeness and coarseness; but the search he was on had humanized what hitherto had only seemed a disagreeable and objectionable side of life, and the people before him were of an odd kinship. In their faces was hunger. There were so many kinds of hunger in the world. He got up, and with a nod to the boy paid his bill and went out.

Through the afternoon hours he walked steadily. Dogged determination made him keep on, just as sensitive shrinking prevented his making inquiries of others. It was silly to ask what couldn't be answered. He must have been mad the night before not to have noticed where he was going, not to have asked Carmencita her name.

By four o'clock the street-lights had been turned on, making of the dark, dingy tenements a long lane with high, unbroken walls, and on a corner he stood for a moment wondering which was the best way to go. To his left were shops; he went toward them, and each face of the children coming in or going out was scanned intently. Seeing a group pressed close to a window in which was displayed an assortment of dolls of all sorts and sizes, with peculiar clothing of peculiar colors, he went toward them, stood for a moment by their side. One of the children was the size of Carmencita.

"That's mine - that one in the pink-silk dress" - a dirty little finger was pointed to a huge and highly decorated doll in the center of the window - "that and the blue beads, and that box of paints with the picture on it, and -"

"You're a pig, all right. Want the earth, don't you? Well, you can't have it." And valiantly a child with a shawl on her head pushed closer to the window, now clouded by the steam from many little mouths. "I want that one - the one in long clothes with a cap on. What you want, Lizzie Lue? Look out there and keep your elbows where they belong" - this to the jostling, pushing crowd behind. "Come on, kid; kick if you have to; only way you can manage some folks. Which one you want, Lizzie Lue?" And a tiny scrap of a child was held up in arms but little bigger than her own.

As Van Landing listened a sudden impulse to take the children in and get for them the things they wanted came over him; then he walked away. If only he could find Carmencita and let her do the buying. Was Christmas like this every year? These children with no chance - was there no one to give them their share of childhood's rights? Settlement workers, churches, schools, charity associations - things of that sort doubtless saw to them. It was not his business. But wasn't it his business? Could it possibly be his business to know - and care?

"I beg your pardon, sir."

Van Landing looked up. A tall, slender man in working-clothes, a basket on one arm, his wife holding to the other, tried to touch his hat. "The crowd makes walking hard without pushing. I hope I didn't step on your foot."

"Didn't touch it." The man had on no overcoat, and his hands were red and chapped. He was much too thin for his height, and as he coughed Van Landing understood. "Shopping, I suppose?"

Why he asked he did not know, and it was the wife he asked, the young wife whose timid clutch of her husband's arm was very unlike the manner of most of the women he had passed. She looked up.

"We were afraid to wait until to-morrow, it's snowing so hard. We might not be able to get out, and the children -"

"We've got three kiddies home." The man's thin face brightened, and he rubbed his coat sleeve across his mouth to check his cough. "Santa Claus is sure enough to them, and we don't want 'em to know different till we have to. A merry Christmas, sir!"

As they went on Van Landing turned and looked. They were poor people. But were they quite so poor as he? He had seen many for whom he might have made Christmas had he known in time - might have saved the sacrifices that had to be made;

but would it then have been Christmas? Slowly, very slowly, in the shabby street and snow-filled air, an understanding of things but dimly glimpsed before was coming to him, and he was seeing what for long had been unseen.

CHAPTER IX

"Think hard, Father - oh, *please* think hard! It was Van - Van - " Carmencita, hands clutched tightly behind her back, leaned forward on her tiptoes and anxiously peered into her father's face for sign of dawning memory. "If I hadn't been so Christmas-crazy I'd have listened better, but I wasn't thinking about his name. Can't you - *can't* you remember the last part? It was Van - Van -"

Slowly her father shook his head. "I wish I could, Carmencita. I don't hear well of late and I didn't catch his name. You called him Mr. Van."

"I called him that for short. I'm a cutting-down person even in names." The palms of Carmencita's hands came together and her fingers interlocked. "If I'd had more sense and manners I'd have called his name right from the first, and we wouldn't have lost him. I could have found him to-day if I'd known what to look for in the telephone-book, or if Miss Frances had been at Mother McNeil's. She might as well be lost, too, but she'll be back at seven, and that's why I am going now, so as to be there the minute she gets in, to ask her what his -"

"She might not like your asking, Carmencita. You must be careful, child. Miss Barbour is not a lady one can -"

"Not a lady one can what?" Carmencita stopped her nervous swaying, and the big blue eyes looked questioningly at her father. "Was there ever a lady who didn't want to find her lost

KATE LANGLEY BOSHER

lover if he was looking for her? That's what he is. And she wants to find him, if she don't know it exactly. She's working it off down here with us children, but she's got something on her mind. He's it. We've got to find him, Father - got to!"

With a dexterous movement of her fingers Carmencita fastened the buttons of her coat and pulled her hat down on her head. "I'm going back to Mother McNeil's," she said, presently, and the large and half-worn rubbers which she had tied on over her shoes were looked at speculatively. "The Damanarkist is going to take me. As soon as Miss Frances tells me Mr. Van's name I'll telephone him to come quick, but I won't tell her that. She might go away again. In that slushy book I read the girl ought to have been shook. She was dying dead in love with her sweetheart and treated him like he was a poodle-dog. Miss Frances wouldn't do that, but I don't know what she might do, and I'm not going to tell her any more than I can help. I want her to think it just happened. Good-by, and go to sleep if you want to, but don't smoke, please. You might drop the sparks on your coat. Good-by."

With a swift kiss she was gone and, meeting the Damanarkist, who was waiting outside the door, they went down the three flights of steps and out into the street. The wind was biting, and, turning up the collar of her coat, Carmencita put her hands in her pockets and made effort to walk rapidly through the thick snow into which her feet sank with each step. For some minutes conversation was impossible. Heads ducked to keep out of their faces the fast-falling flakes, they trudged along in silence until within a few doors of Mother McNeil's house, and then Carmencita looked up.

"Do - do you ever pray, Mr. Leimberg - pray hard, I mean?"

"Pray!" The Damanarkist drew in his breath and laughed with smothered scorn. "Pray! Why should I pray? I cut out prayer when I was a kid. No, I don't pray."

"It's a great comfort, praying is." Carmencita's hand was taken out of her pocket and slipped through the arm of her disillusioned friend. "Sometimes you're just bound to pray. It's like breathing - you can't help it. It - it just rises up. I prayed yesterday for - for something, and it pretty near happened, but -"

"And you think your praying helped to make it happen!" Mr. Leimberg drew Carmencita's hand farther through his arm, and his lips twisted in contemptuous pity. "You think there is a magician up - oh, somewhere, who makes things happen, do you? Think -"

"Yes." Carmencita's feet skipped in spite of the clogging snow. "I think that somewhere there is Somebody who knows about everything, but I don't think He means us to ask for anything we want just because we want it and don't do a lick to get it. I've been praying for months and months about my temper and stamping my foot when I get mad, and if I remember in time and hold down the up-comings my prayers are always answered; but when I let go and forget - " Carmencita whistled a long, low, significant note. "I guess then I don't want to be answered. I want to smash something. But I didn't pray yesterday about tempers and stamping. It was pretty near a miracle that I asked for, though I said I wasn't asking for miracles or -"

"All people who pray ask for miracles. Since the days when men feared floods and famines and pestilence and evil spirits they have cried out for protection and propitiated what to them were gods." The Damanarkist spit upon the ground as if to spew contempt of pretense and cupidity. "I've no patience with it. If there is a God, He knows the cursed struggle life is with most of us; and if there isn't, prayer is but a waste of time."

Carmencita lifted her eyes and for a moment looked in the dark, thin face, embittered by the losing battle of life, as if she had not heard aright, then she laughed softly.

"If I didn't know you, dear Mr. Damanarkist, I'd think you really meant it - what you said. And you don't. I don't guess there's anybody in all the world who doesn't pray sometimes. Something in you does it by itself, and you can't keep it back. You just wait until you feel all lost and lonely and afraid, or so glad you are ready to sing out loud, then you'll do it - inside, if you don't speak out. If I prayed harder to have more sense and not talk so much, and not say what I think about people, and not hate my ugly clothes so, and despise the smell of onions and cabbage and soap-suds, I might get more answers, but you can't get answers just by praying. You've got to work like the mischief, and be a regular policeman over yourself and nab the bad things the minute they poke their heads out. If I'd prayed differently yesterday I wouldn't have been looking for - for somebody all to-day, and be a jumping-jack to-night for fear I won't find him. Did - did you ever have a sweetheart, Mr. Damanarkist?" Before answer could be made Mother McNeil's house was reached, and with steps that were leaps Carmencita was at the door, and a moment later inside. Finding that Miss Frances had returned, she called to Mr. Leimberg to come for her on his way back from the station library where he was to get his book, and breathlessly she ran to Miss Barbour's door and knocked violently upon it.

To the "come in" she entered, eyes big and shining, and cheeks stung into color by the bitter wind; and with a rush forward the hands of her adored friend were caught and held with a tight and nervous grip.

"Miss Frances! Miss Frances!"

Two arms were flung around Miss Barbour's waist, and for a moment the curly brown head was buried on her breast and words refused to come; instead came breathing short and quick; then Carmencita looked up.

"What - oh, what is his name, Miss Frances? He was found and now is lost, and I promised - I promised I'd get you for him!"

Frances Barbour lifted the excited little face and kissed it. "What's the matter, Carmencita? You look as if you'd seen a ghost, and you're talking as if -"

"I'm crazy - I'm not. And there isn't any time to lose. He said he *must* find you before Christmas. There isn't a soul to make Christmas for him, and he hasn't anybody to buy things for, and he's as lonely as a - a desert person, and he doesn't want any one but you. Oh, Miss Frances, what is his name?"

Frances Barbour leaned back in the chair in which she had taken her seat, and her face whitened. "What are you talking about, and who is -"

"I'm talking about - Him." On her knees Carmencita crouched against her friend's chair, and her long, slender fingers intertwined with those which had suddenly grown nerveless. "I'm talking about your sweetheart, Miss Frances. I found him for you, and then I lost him. I'll tell you how it happened after I know all of his name and - If you had seen his face when I told him I knew you and knew where you lived you'd hurry, you'd -"

"If he wishes to see me, why doesn't he - I mean -" Sudden color surged into the face turned from the child's eager eyes. "What are we talking about, Carmencita? There is evidently some mistake."

"There is. An awful one. It's three years old. And we're talking about the gentleman Father and I met yesterday and lost last night. You're his sweetheart, and he wants you for Christmas and for ever after, and he may be dead by to-morrow if he doesn't find you. He came to our house, and I wrote you a note to come, too, and when you didn't do it he looked as if he'd been hit in the face and couldn't breathe good, and he stumbled down the steps like a blind man, and we'd forgot to tell him our name, and he didn't know the number of our house, and -"

She paused for breath and brushed back the curls from her face. "I know he's been looking all day. Where does he live, Miss Frances, and what is his name?"

"If you will tell me of whom you are talking I will tell you whether or not I know him. Until you do -"

"I told you I didn't remember any of his name but the Van part. Don't you know the name of the person you love best on earth? It's his name I want."

Frances Barbour got up and walked over to the bureau and opened its top drawer. "You are asking questions that in any one else I would not permit, Carmencita. I am sure you do not mean to be -"

"I don't mean anything but that I want to know all of Mr. Van's name, and if you don't tell me you are not a Christian!"

With a change of expression Carmencita sprang to her feet and, hands clasped behind her back, she stood erect, her eyes blazing with indignation. "If you don't tell him where you are, don't let him come, I'll think it's all just make-believe and put on, your coming and doing for people you don't really and truly know, and doing nothing for those you do, and letting the ones you love best be lonely and miserable and having Christmas all by themselves when they're starving hungry for you. What is his name?" Carmencita's voice was high and shrill, and her foot was stamped vehemently. "What is his name?"

"Stephen Van Landing."

Face to face, Frances Barbour and Carmencita looked into each other's eyes, then with a leap Carmencita was out of the room and down the steps and at the telephone. With hands that trembled she turned the pages of the book she was holding upside down, then with disgust at her stupidity she righted it and ran her finger down the long line of V's. Finding at last the name she wanted, she called the number, then closed her eyes and prayed fervently, feverishly, and half-aloud the words came jerkily:

"O God, please let him be home, and let him get down here quick before Miss Frances goes out. She and Mother McNeil are going somewhere and won't be back until eleven, and that would be too late for him to come, and - Hello!" The receiver was jammed closer to her ear. "Is that Mr. Van Landing's house? Is he home? He - he - isn't home!" The words came in a little wail. "Oh, he must be home! Are you sure - *sure*? Where can I get him? Where is he? You don't know - hasn't been at the office all day and hasn't telephoned? He's looking - I mean I guess he's, trying to find somebody. Who is this talking? It's - it's a friend of his, and tell him the minute he comes in to call up Pelham 4293 and ask for Miss Frances Barbour, who wants to talk to him. And listen. Tell him if she's out to come to 14 Custer Street, to Mother McNeil's, and wait until she gets home. Write it down. Got it? Yes, that's it. Welcome. Good-by."

The receiver was hung upon its hook, and for a moment Carmencita stared at the wall; then her face sobered. The strain and tension of the day gave way, and the high hopes of the night before went out as at the snuffing of a candle. Presently she nodded into space.

"I stamped my foot at Miss Frances. *Stamped my foot*! And I got mad, and was impertinent, and talked like a gutter girl to a sure-enough lady. Talked like -"

Her teeth came down on her lips to stop their sudden quivering, and the picture on the wall grew blurred and indistinct.

"There isn't any use in praying." Two big tears rolled down her cheeks and fell upon her hands. "I might as well give up."

CHAPTER X

For a half-moment after Carmencita left the room Frances Barbour stood in the middle of the floor and stared at the door, still open, then went over and closed it. Coming back to the table at which she had been writing, she sat down and took up her pen and made large circles on the sheet of paper before her. Slowly the color in her face cooled and left it white.

Carmencita was by nature cyclonic. Her buoyancy and bubbling spirits, her enthusiasms and intensities, were well understood, but how could she possibly know Stephen Van Landing? All day he had been strangely on her mind, always he was in her heart, but thought of him was forced to be subconscious, for none other was allowed. Of late, however, crowd it back as she would, a haunting sense of his presence had been with her, and under the busy and absorbed air with which she had gone about the day's demands there had been sharp surge of unpermitted memories of which she was impatient and ashamed.

Also there had been disquieting questions, questions to which she had long refused to listen, and in the crush and crowd they had pursued her, peered at her in unexpected places, and faced her in the quiet of her room, and from them she was making effort to escape when Carmencita burst in upon her. The latter was too excited, too full of some new adventure, to talk clearly or coherently. Always Carmencita was adventuring, but what could she mean by demanding to know the name of her sweetheart, and by saying she had found him and then lost him? And why had she, Frances Barbour, told her as obediently as if their positions were reversed and she the child instead of Carmencita?

Elbow on the table and chin in the palm of her hand, she tapped the desk-pad with her pen and made small dots in the large circles she had drawn on the paper, and slowly she wrote a name upon it.

What could Stephen Van Landing be doing in this part of the town? He was one of the city's successful men, but he did not know his city. Disagreeable sights and sounds had by him been hitherto avoided, and in this section they were chiefly what was found. Why should he have come to it? That he was selfish and absorbed in his own affairs, that he was conventional and tradition - trained, was as true to-day, perhaps, as when she had told him so three years ago, but had they taught him nothing, these three years that were past? Did he still think, still believe -

With a restless movement she turned in her chair, and her hands twisted in her lap. Was she not still as stubborn as of old, still as proud and impatient of restraint where her sense of freedom and independence of action were in question, still as self-willed? And was it true, what Carmencita had said - was she giving herself to others and refusing herself to the only one who had the right to claim her, the royal right of love?

But how did she know he still needed her, wanted her? When she had returned to her own city after long absence she had told of her present place of residence to but few of her old friends. Her own sorrow, her own sudden facing of the inevitable and unescapable, had brought her sharply to a realization of how little she was doing with the time that was hers, and she had been honest and sincere when she had come to Mother McNeil's and asked to be shown the side of life she had hitherto known but little - the sordid, sinful, struggling side in which children especially had so small a chance. In these years of absence he had made no sign. Even if it were true, what Carmencita had said, that he - that is, a man named Van Something - was looking for her, until he found her she could not tell him where she was.

She had not wished her friends to know. Settlements and society were as oil and water, and for the present the work she had undertaken needed all her time and thought. If only people knew, if only people understood, the things that she now knew and had come to understand, the inequalities and injustices of life would no longer sting and darken and embitter as they stung and darkened and embittered now, and if she and Stephen could work together -

He was living in the same place, his offices were in the same place, and he worked relentlessly, she was told. Although he did not know she was in the city, she knew much of him, knew of his practical withdrawal from the old life, knew of a certain cynicism that was becoming settled; and a thousand times she had blamed herself for the unhappiness that was his as well as hers. She loved her work, would always be glad that she had lived among the people who were so singularly like those other people who thought themselves so different, but if he still needed her, wanted her, was it not her duty -

With an impatient movement of her hands she got up and went over to the window. There was no duty about it. It was love that called him to her. She should not have let Carmencita go without finding from her how it happened that she had met Stephen Van Landing on Custer Street. She must go to Carmencita and ask her. If he were really looking for her they might spend Christmas together. The blood surged hotly to her face, and the beating of her heart made her hands unsteady. If together -

A noise behind made her turn. Hand on the door-knob, Carmencita was standing in the hall, her head inside the room. All glow was gone, and hope and excitement had yielded to dejection and despair.

"I just came to beg your pardon for - for stamping my foot, and I'm sorry I said what I did." The big blue eyes looked down on the floor and one foot twisted around the other. "It isn't any use to forgive me. I'm not worth forgiving. I'm not worth -"

The door was slammed violently, and before Miss Barbour could reach the hall Carmencita was down the steps and out into the street, where the Damanarkist was waiting.

CHAPTER XI

Late into the night Stephen Van Landing kept up his hurried walking. Again and again he had stopped and made inquiries of policemen, of children, of men and women, but no one knew that of which he asked. A blind man who played the harp, a child named Carmencita, a boy called Noodles, a settlement house, he supposed, over which Mother Somebody presided - these were all he had to go on. To ask concerning Miss Barbour was impossible. He could not bring himself to call her name. He would have to go to headquarters for help. To-morrow would be Christmas eve. He *would not* spend Christmas alone - or in the usual way.

"Say, mister, don't you wish you was a boy again? Get out the way!"

With a push the boy swept by him, pulling on a self-constructed sleigh a still smaller boy, and behind the two swarmed a bunch of yelling youngsters who, as they passed, pelted him with snow. One of them stopped to tie the string of his shoe, and, looking down, Van Landing saw - Noodles.

With a swift movement he reached down to grab him, but, thinking it was a cop, the boy was up and gone with a flash and in half a moment was out of sight. As swiftly as the boy Van Landing ran down the street and turned the corner he had seen the boy turn. His heart was beating thickly, his breath came unevenly, and the snow was blinding, but there was no thought of stopping. He bumped into a man coming toward him, and two hats flew in the air and on the pavement, but he went on. The hat did not matter, only Noodles mattered, and Noodles could no longer be seen. Down the street, around first one corner and then another, he kept on in fierce pursuit for some moments; then, finding breathing difficult, he paused and leaned against the step railing of a high porch, to better get his bearings. Disappointment and fury were overmastering him. It was impossible and absurd to have within one's grasp what one had been looking for all day and part of two nights, and have it slip away like that.

"Come on. No use - that -" The policeman's voice was surly. "If you'll walk quiet I won't ring up. If you don't you'll get a free ride. Come on."

"Come on?" Van Landing put his hand to his head. His hat was gone. He looked down at his feet. They were soaking wet. His overcoat was glazed with a coating of fine particles of ice, and his hands were trembling. He had eaten practically nothing since his lunch of Tuesday, had walked many miles, and slept but a few hours after a night of anxious searching, and suddenly he felt faint and sick.

"Come on?" he repeated. "Come where?"

"Where you belong." The policeman's grasp was steadying. "Hurry up. I can't wait here all night."

"Neither can I." Van Landing took out his handkerchief and wiped his face. "I wish you'd get my hat." The crowd was pressing closer. He was losing time and must get away. Besides, he could not trust himself. The man's manner was insolent, and he was afraid he would kick him. Instead he slipped some money in his hand.

"Mistake, my friend. You'd have your trouble for nothing if you took me in. There's no charge save running. I want to find a boy who passed me just now. Name is Noodles. Know him?"

For a moment the cop hesitated. The man's voice, dress, manner, were not the sort seen in this section, and the bill slipped in his hand had a yellow tinge - still -

"I've dropped my hat. Get it, will you?" Van Landing threw some change in the still gathering crowd, and as they scampered for it he turned to the policeman, then caught hold of the railing. A hateful faintness was coming over him again. On the edge of the crowd a girl with a middle-aged woman had stopped, and the girl was making her way toward him.

"What is it, Mr. Cronklin? Not one of our boys?" The clear voice reached him as if at his side. He steadied himself, stared, and tried to speak.

"Frances," he said, and held out his hands. "You've made me walk so far, Frances, and Christmas is -"

In the snow his feet slipped. The cop was such a fool. He had never fainted in his life.

Some one was standing near him. Who was it, and where was he? This wasn't his room. On his elbow, he looked around. Nothing was familiar. It must be a woman's room; he could see photographs and a pin-cushion on the bureau, and flowers were growing on a table near the window. The bed he was in was small and white. His was big and brass. What had happened? Slowly it came to him, and he started to get up, then fell back. The surge of blood receded, and again there was giddiness. Had he lost her? Had she, too, slipped out of his hands because of his confounded fall? It was a durned outrage that he should have fallen. Who was that man with his back to the bed?

The man turned. "All right, are you? That's good!" His pulse was felt with professional fingers, but in the doctor's voice was frank interest. "You were pretty nearly frozen, man. It's well she saw you."

"Where is she?" Van Landing sat up. "Where are my clothes? I must get up."

"I guess not." The doctor laughed, but his tone was as decisive as his act. Van Landing was pushed back on the pillow and the covering pulled up. "Do you mean Miss Barbour?"

"Yes. Where is Miss Barbour?"

The doctor wrote something on a slip of paper. "Down-stairs, waiting to hear how you are. I'll go down and tell her. I'll see you in the morning."

"Where am I? Whose house is this?"

"Your house at present." The doctor laughed again. "It's Mother McNeil's house, but all who need it use it, and you needed it, all right. You struck your head on the bottom step of the porch three doors from here. Had it been an inch nearer the temple - Pretty bad knock-out, as it was, but you'll be all right to-morrow. If you wake up in a couple of hours take another one of these" - a pill was obediently swallowed - "but you're to see no one until I see you again. No talking."

"Sorry, but I must see Miss Barbour." In Van Landing's voice was sharp fear. "Christmas isn't over yet? I haven't missed it, have I? Are you sure she's in this house?"

"Sure. She's getting ready for to-morrow. To-morrow will be the busiest day in the year. It's Christmas eve."

Van Landing slipped down in the bed and his face went deep in the pillows. Reaction was on. A horrible fear that he was going to cry, going to do some abominably childish thing, made him stuff the covering in his mouth and press his feet hard against the foot of the bed. He would *not* be cheated out of Christmas! He had believed he hated it, thought he wanted to be dead during it, and now if it were over and nothing done - Presently he spoke.

"Will you ask Miss Barbour if I may speak to her in the morning - before she goes out? My name is Van Landing - Stephen Van Landing. I was a friend of hers once."

"One now." The doctor's voice was dryly emphatic. "Lucky she recognized you. Rather startled her, finding an old friend so unexpectedly." Over his spectacles his kind, shrewd eyes looked down on the man in the bed. "I'll see her. Miss Barbour is an exceptional woman, but she's a woman, which means when she knows you are all right she may not have time to see you. At present she's outside your door. That's her knock. Guess she's got the milk."

With breath held, Van Landing listened. Very low were the words spoken, then the door was closed again. His heart was calling to her. The long and empty years in which he had hoped against hope, and yet could make no effort to find her, faded as mist fades before the light that dawns and glows; and to say no word when she was near, to hold hands still that longed to outstretch, to make no sign when he would kneel for pardon at her feet - it was not to be endured. He would not wait; the doctor must let her in!

But it was not the doctor who was at his bed. It was a short, plump woman of more than middle age, with twinkling gray eyes and firm, kind hands and a cheery voice.

"It's the milk, my son," she said, and the steaming glass was held to his lips. "When you've had it you will sleep like a baby. It's warm, are you - and the feet good and hot? Let me feel that water-bag? Bless my soul if it's even lukewarm, and your feet still shivery! It's no wonder, for they were ice itself when they brought you in."

With dexterous fingers the hot-water bag was withdrawn from the foot of the bed and Mother McNeil was out of the room. Back again, she slipped it close to his feet, tucked in the covering, patted the pillows, and, lowering the light, turned to leave the room. At the door she stopped.

"Is there anything you're needing, my son - anything I can do for you?"

For a moment there was silence, broken only by the ticking of a tiny clock on the mantel, then Van Landing spoke.

"Yes." His voice was boyishly low. "Will you ask Miss Barbour if I may see her to-morrow before she goes out? I *must* see her."

"Of course I will. And you can tell her how it happened that you were right near our door when you fell, and you didn't even know she was in town. Very few of her up-town friends know. There wasn't time for both up-town and down-town, and there were things she wanted to find out. She tells me you are an old friend, and I'm glad you've come across each other again. It pleases some folks to believe in chance, but I get more comfort thinking God has His own way. Good night, Mr. Van Landing. Good dreams - good dreams!"

The door was closed softly, and under the bedclothes Van Landing again buried his face in the pillows, and his lips twitched. Chance - was it chance or was it God? If only God would give him a chance!

CHAPTER XII

He was too tired, too utterly relaxed by warmth and medicine, to think clearly. To-morrow he would find Carmencita, and she should get the things the children wanted. They were very strange, the places and people he had seen to-day. Of course he had known about such places and people, read about them, heard about them, but seeing for one's self was different. There were a lot of bummers among these people he had passed; much of their misery was of their own making (he had made much of his), but the wonder was they were no worse.

Bold, bad faces, cold, pinched, hungry ones, eager, earnest, pathetic and joyous, worn and weary, burdened and care-free, they again passed before him, misty and ill-defined, as though the snow still veiled and made them hazy, and none of them he knew. He wished they would stop passing. He was very tired. They, too, were tired. Would they for ever be passing before him, these people, these little children, he had seen to-day? If they would go away he could think more clearly, could think of Frances. She was here, in the house with him. At first it had seemed strange, but it wasn't strange. It would be strange if she were not here when he needed her, wanted her so. To-morrow would not be too late. One could do a good deal on Christmas eve. Everybody had been busy except himself. He would telephone to-morrow and tell Herrick to close the office and give Miss Davis holiday until after New-Year.

But she had nowhere to go. He had heard her tell Herrick so, and Herrick had nowhere to go, either. Both lived in boarding-houses, he supposed. He had never thought to ask. Herrick was a faithful old plodder - never would be anything else - but he couldn't get on without him. He ought to raise his salary. Why didn't Herrick ask for more money if he wanted it? And then he could get married. Why didn't he get married, anyhow? Once or twice he had seen him talking to Miss Davis about something that evidently wasn't business. She was a pretty little thing and quick as lightning - just the opposite of old Herrick. Wouldn't it be funny if they were in love; not, of course, like -

They had nowhere to go Christmas. If Frances would let them they might come here - no, not here, but at his home, their home. His home was Frances's. It wouldn't be home for him if it weren't for her also. He would ask her. And Carmencita and her blind father, they could come, too. It would be horrible to have a Christmas dinner of sardines or toasted cheese and crackers - or one in a boarding-house. Other people might think it queer that he should have accidentally met Carmencita, and that Carmencita should have mentioned the name of Miss Barbour, and that he should have walked miles and miles - it must have been thousands of miles - trying to find her, and, after all, did not find her. She found him. But it wasn't queer. He had been looking for her ever since - for three years he had been looking for her, and what one looks for long enough one always finds. To-morrow - to-morrow - would - be - Christmas eve.

He opened his eyes slowly. The sun was blinding, and he blinked. Mother McNeil and the doctor were standing at the foot of the bed, and as he rubbed his eyes they laughed.

"It's a merry Christmas you're to have, my son, after all, and it's wanting to be up and after it you are, if I'm a judge of looks." And Van Landing's hand, holding the coverlid close to his neck, was patted understandingly by Mother McNeil. "Last night the doctor was a bit worried about your head - you took your time in coming to - but I didn't believe it was as bad as he feared, and it's well it wasn't, for it's a grand day in which to be living, and you'll need your head. Is it coffee or tea, now, that you like best for breakfast? And an egg and a bit of toast, doctor, I think will taste well. I'll get them." And without answer Mother McNeil was gone.

The doctor sat down, felt his patient's pulse, took his temperature, investigated the cut on the forehead, then got up. "You're all right." His tone was one of gruff relief. "One inch nearer your temple, however - You can get up if you wish. Good day." And he, too, was gone before Van Landing could ask a question or say a word of thanks.

It was bewildering, perplexing, embarrassing, and for a moment he hesitated. Then he got up. He was absurdly shaky, but his head was clear, and in his heart humility that was new and sweet. The day was great, and the sun was shining as on yesterday one would not have dreamed it could ever shine again. Going over to the door, he locked it and hurriedly began to dress. His clothes had a rough, dry appearance that made them hardly recognizable, and to get on his shoes, which evidently had been dried near the furnace, was difficult. In the small mirror over the bureau, as he tied his cravat, his face reflected varying emotions: disgust at his soiled collar, relief that he was up again, and gratitude that made a certain cynicism, of late becoming too well defined, fade into quiet purpose.

Unlocking the door, he went back to the window and looked across at the long row of houses, as alike as shriveled peas in a dry pod, and down on the snow-covered streets. Brilliantly the sun touched here and there a bit of cornice below a dazzling gleaming roof, and threw rays of rainbow light on window-pane and iron rail, outlined or hidden under frozen foam; and the dirt and ugliness of the usual day were lost in the white hush of mystery.

Not for long would there be transforming effect of the storm, however. Already the snow was being shoveled from door-steps and sidewalks, and the laughter of the boys as they worked, the scraping of their shovels, the rumble of wagon-wheels, which were making deep brown ruts in the middle of the street, reached him with the muffled sound of something far away, and, watching, he missed no detail of what was going on below.

"Goodness gracious! I've almost cried myself to death! And she found you - found you!"

Van Landing turned sharply. The door was open, though he had not heard the knock, and with a spring Carmencita was beside him, holding his hands and dancing as if demented with a joy no longer to be held in restraint.

"Oh, Mr. Van, I've almost died for fear I wouldn't find you in time! And you're here at Mother McNeil's, and all yesterday I looked and looked, and I couldn't remember your last name, and neither could Father. And Miss Frances was away until night, and I never prayed so hard and looked so hard in my life! Oh, Mr. Van, if you are a stranger, I love you, and I'm so glad you're found!"

She stopped for breath, and Van Landing, stooping, lifted Carmencita's face and kissed it.

"You are my dear friend, Carmencita." His voice, as his hands, was a bit shaky. "I, too, am very glad - and grateful. Will you ask her to come, ask her to let me see her? I cannot wait any longer."

"You'll have to." Carmencita's eyes were big and blue in sudden seriousness. "The Little Big Sisters have their tree to-night, and she's got a million trillion things to do to-day, and she's gone out. She's awful glad you're better, though. I asked her, and she said she was. And I asked her why she didn't marry you right straight away, or to-morrow if she didn't have time to-day, and -"

"You did what, Carmencita?"

"That. I asked her that. What's the use of wasting time? I told her you'd like a wife for a Christmas gift very much, if she was the wife. Wouldn't you? Wouldn't you really and truly rather have her than anything else?"

Van Landing turned and looked out of the window. The child's eyes and earnest, eager face could not be met in the surge of hot blood which swept over him, and his throat grew tight. All his theories and ideas were becoming but confused upheaval in the manipulations of fate, or what you will, that were bringing strange things to pass, and he no longer could think clearly or feel calmly. He must get away before he saw Frances.

"Wouldn't you, Mr. Van?"

In the voice beside him was shy entreaty and appeal, and, hands clasped behind her, Carmencita waited.

"I would." Van Landing made effort to smile, but in his eyes was no smiling. Into them had come sudden purpose. "I shall ask her to marry me to-morrow."

Arms extended to the limit of their length, Carmencita whirled round and round the room, then, breathless, stopped and, taking Van Landing's hand, lifted it to her lips.

"I kiss your hand, my lord, and bring you greetings from your faithful subjects! I read that in a book. I'll be the subject. Isn't it grand and magnificent and glorious?" She stopped. "She hasn't any new clothes. A lady can't get married without new clothes, can she? And she won't have time to get any on Christmas eve. Whether she'll do it or not, you'll have to make her, Mr. Van, or you'll lose her again. You've - got - to - just - make - her!"

Carmencita's long slender forefinger made a jab in Van Landing's direction, and her head nodded with each word uttered. But before he could answer, Mother McNeil, with breakfast on a tray, was in the room and Carmencita was out.

Sitting down beside him, as he asked her to do, Van Landing told her how it happened he was there, told her who he was. Miss Barbour was under her care. She had once been his promised wife. He was trying to find her when he fell, or fainted, or whatever it was, that he might ask her again to marry him. Would she help him?

In puzzled uncertainty Mother McNeil had listened, fine little folds wrinkling her usually smooth forehead, and her keen eyes searching the face before her; then she got up.

"I might have known it would end like this. Well, why not?" Hands on her hips, she smiled in the flushed face looking into hers. Van Landing had risen, and his hands, holding the back of his chair, twitched badly. "The way of love is the way of life. If she will marry you - God bless you, I will say. It's women like Frances the work we're in is needing. But it's women like her that men need, too. She's out, but she asked me to wish you a very happy Christmas."

CHAPTER XIII

"A very happy Christmas!" Van Landing smiled. "How can I have it without - When can I see her, Mother McNeil?"

At the open door Mother McNeil turned. "She has some shopping to do. Yesterday two more families were turned over to us. Sometimes she gets lunch at the Green Tea-pot on Samoset Street. She will be home at four. The children come at eight, and the tree is to be dressed before they get here." A noise made her look around. "Carmencita, - you are out of breath, child! It's never you will learn to walk, I'm fearing!"

Carmencita, who had run down the hall as one pursued, stopped, pulled up her stocking, and made effort to fasten it to its supporter. "Christmas in my legs," she said. "Can't expect feet to walk on Christmas eve. I've got to tell him something, Mother McNeil. Will you excuse me, please, if I tell him by himself?"

Coming inside the room, Carmencita pulled Van Landing close to her and closed the door, and for half a minute paused for breath.

"It was Her. It was Miss Barbour at the telephone, and she says I must meet her at the Green Tea-pot at two o'clock and have lunch with her and tell her about the Barlow babies and old Miss Parker and some others who don't go to Charities for their Christmas - and she says I can help buy the things. Glory! I'm glad I'm living!" She stopped. "I didn't tell her a word about you, but - Have you got a watch?"

Van Landing looked at his watch, then put it back. "I have a watch, but no hat. I lost my hat last night chasing Noodles. It's nine o'clock. I'm going to the Green Tea-pot at two to take lunch also. Want to go with me?"

"I'm not going with you. You are going with me." Carmencita made effort to look tall. "That's what I came to tell you. And you can ask her there. I won't listen. I won't even look, and -"

Van Landing took up his overcoat, hesitated, and then put it on. "I've never had a sure-enough Christmas, Carmencita. Why can't I get those things for the kiddies you spoke of, and save Miss Barbour the trouble? She has so much to do, it isn't fair to put more on her. Then, too -"

"You can have her by yourself after we eat, can't you? Where can you go?"

"I haven't thought yet. Where do you suppose? She ought to rest."

"Rest!" Carmencita's voice was shrilly scornful. "Rest - on Christmas eve. Besides, there isn't a spot to do it in. Every one has bundles in it." Hands clasped, her forehead puckered in fine folds, then she looked up. "Is - is it a nice house you live in? It's all right, isn't it?"

"It is considered so. Why?"

"Because what's the use of waiting until to-morrow to get married? If she'll have you you all could stop in that little church near the Green Tea-pot and the man could marry you, and then she could go on up to your house and rest while you finished your Christmas things, and then you could go for her and bring her down here to help fix the Christmas tree, and to-morrow you could have Christmas at home. Wouldn't it be grand?" Carmencita was on tiptoe, and again her arms were flung in the air. Poised as if for flight, her eyes were on the ceiling. Her voice changed. "The roof of this house leaks. It ought to be fixed."

Van Landing opened the door. "Your plan is an excellent one, Carmencita. I like it immensely, but there's a chance that Miss Barbour may not agree. Women have ways of their own in matters of marriage. I do not even know that she will marry me at all."

"Then she's got mighty little sense, which isn't so, for she's got a lot. She knows what she wants, all right, and if she likes you she likes you, and if she don't, she don't, and she don't make out she does. Did - did you fuss?"

"We didn't fuss." Van Landing smiled slightly. "We didn't agree about certain things."

"Good gracious! You don't want to marry an agree-er, do you? Mrs. Barlow's one. Everything her husband thinks, she thinks, too, and sometimes he can't stand her another minute. Where are you going now?"

"I'm going to telephone for a taxi-cab. Then I'm going home to change my clothes and get a hat, and then I'm going to my office to look after some matters there; then I'm going with you to do some shopping, and then I'm going to the Green Tea-pot to meet Miss Barbour. If you could go with me now it would save time. Can you go?"

"If I can tell Father first. Wait for me, will you?"

Around the corner Carmencita flew, and was back as the taxi-cab stopped at Mother McNeil's door. Getting in, she sat upright and shut her eyes. Van Landing was saying good-by and expressing proper appreciation and mentally making notes of other forms of expression to be made later; and as she waited her breath came in long, delicious gasps through her half-parted lips. Presently she stooped over and pinched her legs.

"My legs," she said, "same ones. And my cheeks and my hair" - the latter was pulled with vigor - "and my feet and my hands - all me, and in a taxi-cab going Christmas shopping and maybe to a marriage, and I didn't know he was living last week! Father says I mustn't speak to people I don't know, but how can you know them if you don't speak? I was born lucky, and I'm so glad I'm living that if I was a rooster I'd crow. Oh, Mr. Van, are you ready?"

The next few hours to Carmencita were the coming true of dreams that had long been denied, and from one thrill to another she passed in a delicious ecstasy which made pinching of some part of her body continually necessary. While Van Landing dressed she waited in his library, wandering in wide-eyed awe and on tiptoe from one part of the room to the other, touching here and there with the tips of her fingers a book or picture or piece of furniture, and presently in front of a footstool she knelt down and closed her eyes.

Quickly, however, she opened them and, with head on the side, looked around and listened. This wasn't a time to be seen. The silence assuring, she again shut her eyes very tight and the palms of her hands, uplifted, were pressed together.

"Please, dear God, I just want to thank you," she began. "It's awful sudden and unexpected having a day like this, and I don't guess to-morrow will be much, not a turkey Christmas or anything like that, but to-day is grand. I'd say more, but some one is coming. Amen." And with a scramble she was on her feet, the stool behind her, as Van Landing came in the room.

The ride to the office through crowded streets was breathlessly thrilling, and during it Carmencita did not speak. At the window of the taxi she pressed her face so closely that the glass had continually to be wiped lest the cloud made by her breath prevent her seeing clearly; and, watching her, Van Landing

KATE LANGLEY BOSHER

smiled. What an odd, elfish, wistful little face it was - keen, alert, intelligent, it reflected every emotion that filled her, and her emotions were many. In her long, ill-fitting coat and straw hat, in the worn shoes and darned gloves, she was a study that puzzled and perplexed, and at thought of her future he frowned. What became of them - these children with little chance? Was it to try and learn and help that Frances was living in their midst?

In his office Herrick and Miss Davis were waiting. Work had been pretty well cleared up, and there was little to be done, and as Van Landing saw them the memory of his half-waking, half-dreaming thought concerning them came to him, and furtively he looked from one to the other.

In a chair near the window, hands in her lap and feet on the rounds, Carmencita waited, her eyes missing no detail of the scene about her, and at Miss Davis, who came over to talk to her, she looked with frank admiration. For a moment there was hesitating uncertainty in Van Landing's face; then he turned to Herrick.

"Come into the next room, will you, Herrick? I want to speak to you a minute."

What he was going to say he did not know. Herrick was such a steady old chap, from him radiated such uncomplaining patience, about him was such aloofness concerning his private affairs, that to speak to him on personal matters was difficult. He handed him cigars and lighted one himself.

"I'm going to close the office, Herrick, until after New-Year," he began. "I thought perhaps you might like to go away."

"I would." Herrick, whose cigar was unlighted, smiled slightly. "But I don't think I'll go."

"Why not?"

Herrick hesitated, and his face flushed. He was nearing forty, and his hair was already slightly gray. "There are several reasons," he said, quietly. "Until I am able to be married I do not care to go away. She would be alone, and Christmas alone -"

"Is - is it Miss Davis, Herrick?" Van Landing's voice was strangely shy; then he held out his hand. "You're a lucky man, Herrick. I congratulate you. Why didn't you tell me before; and if you want to get married, why not? What's the use of waiting? The trip's on me. Christmas alone - I forgot to say I've intended for some time to raise your salary. You deserve it, and it was thoughtlessness that made me put it off." He sat down at his desk and took his check-book out of a spring-locked drawer and wrote hastily upon it. "That may help to start things, Herrick, and if there's any other way -"

In Herrick's astonished face the blood pumped deep and red, and as he took the check Van Landing put in his hands his fingers twitched nervously. It was beyond belief that Van Landing should have guessed - and the check! It would mean the furnishing of the little flat they had looked at yesterday and hoped would stay unrented for a few months longer; meant a trip, and a little put aside to add to their slow savings. Now that his sister was married and his brother out of school, he could save more, but with this - He tried to speak, then turned away and walked over to the window.

"Call her in, Herrick, and let's have it settled. Why not get the license to-day and be married to-morrow? Oh, Miss Davis!" He opened the door and beckoned to his stenographer, who was showing Carmencita her typewriter. "Come in, will you? Never mind. We'll come in there."

CHAPTER XIV

Miss Davis, who had risen, stood with one hand on her desk; the other went to her lips. Something was the matter. What was it?

"I hope you won't mind Carmencita knowing." Van Landing drew the child to him. "She is an admirable arranger and will like to help, I'm sure. Miss Davis and Mr. Herrick are going to be married to-morrow, Carmencita, and spend their holiday - wherever they choose. Why, Miss Davis - why, you've never done like this before!"

Miss Davis was again in her chair, and, with arms on her desk and face buried in them, her shoulders were making little twitchy movements. She was trying desperately hard to keep back something that mustn't be heard, and in a flash Carmencita was on her knees beside her.

"Oh, Miss Davis, I don't know you much, but I'm so glad, and of course it's awful exciting to get married without knowing you're going to do it; but you mustn't cry, Miss Davis - you mustn't, really!"

"I'm not crying." Head up, the pretty brown eyes, wet and shining, looked first at Herrick and then at Van Landing, and a handkerchief wiped two quivering lips. "I'm not crying, only - only it's so sudden, and to-morrow is Christmas, and a boarding-house Christmas -" Again the flushed face was buried in her arms and tears came hot and fast - happy, blinding tears.

Moving chairs around that were not in the way, going to the window and back again, locking up what did not require locking, putting on his hat and taking it off without knowing what he was doing, Van Landing, nevertheless, managed in an incredibly short time to accomplish a good many things and to make practical arrangements. Herrick and Miss Davis were to come to his apartment at one o'clock to-morrow and bring the minister. They would be married at once and have dinner immediately after with him - and with a friend or two, perhaps. Carmencita and her father would also be there, and they could leave for a trip as soon as they wished. They must hurry; there was no time to lose - not a minute.

With a few words to the office-boy, the elevator-boy, the janitor, and additional remembrances left with the latter for the charwoman, the watchman, and several others not around, they were out in the street and Carmencita again helped in the cab.

For a moment there was dazed silence, then she turned to Van Landing. "Would you mind sticking this in me?" she asked, and handed him a bent pin. "Is - is it really sure-enough what we've been doing, or am I making up. Stick hard, please - real hard."

Van Landing laughed. "No need for the pin." He threw it away. "You're awake, all right. I've been asleep a long time, and you - have waked me, Carmencita."

For two delicious hours the child led and Van Landing followed. In and out of stores they went with quickness and decision, and soon on the seat and on the floor of the cab boxes and bundles of many shapes and sizes were piled, and then Carmencita said there should be nothing else.

"It's awful wickedness, Mr. Van, to spend so much." Her head nodded vigorously. "The children will go crazy, and so will their mothers, and they'll pop open if they eat some of all the things you've bought for them, and we mustn't get another one. It's been grand, but - You're not drunk, are you, Mr. Van, and don't know what you're doing?"

Her voice trailed off anxiously, and in her eyes came sudden, sober fear.

Again Van Landing laughed. "I think perhaps I am drunk, but not in the way you mean, Carmencita. It's a matter of spirits, however. Something has gone to my head, or perhaps it's my heart. But I know very well what I'm doing. There's one thing more. I forgot to tell you. I have a little friend who has done a good deal for me. I want to get her a present or two - some clothes and things that girls like. Your size, I think, would fit her. I'd like -"

"Is she rich or poor?"

Van Landing hesitated. "She is rich. She has a wonderful imagination and can see all sorts of things that others don't see, and her friends are -"

"Kings and queens, and fairies and imps, and ghosts and devils. I know. I've had friends like that. Does she like pink or blue?"

"I think she likes - blue." Again Van Landing hesitated. Silks and satins might be Carmencita's choice. Silks and satins would not do. "I don't mean she has money, and I believe she'd rather have practical things."

"No, she wouldn't! Girls hate practical things." The long, loose, shabby coat was touched lightly. "This is practical. Couldn't she have one pair of shiny slippers, just one, with buckles on them? Maybe she's as Cinderellary as I am. I'd rather stick my foot out with a diamond-buckle slipper on it than eat. I do when my princess friends call, and they always say: 'Oh, Carmencita, what a charming foot you have!' And that's it. *That!*" And Carmencita's foot with it's coarse and half-worn shoe was held out at full length. "But we've got to hurry, or we won't be at the Green Tea-pot by two o'clock.

Come on."

With amazing discrimination Carmencita made her purchases, and only once or twice did she overstep the limitations of practicality and insist upon a present that could be of little use to its recipient. For the giving of joy the selection of a pair of shining slippers, a blue satin sash, and a string of amber beads were eminently suitable, however, and, watching, Van Landing saw her eyes gleam over the precious possessions she was supposedly buying for some one else, a child of her own age, and he made no objection to the selections made.

"Even if she don't wear them she will have them." And Carmencita drew a long, deep sigh of satisfaction. "It's so nice to know you have got something you can peep at every now and then. It's like eating when you're hungry. Oh, I do hope she'll like them! Is it two, Mr. Van?"

It was ten minutes to two, and, putting Carmencita into the bundle-packed cab, Van Landing ordered the latter to the Green Tea-pot, then, getting in, leaned back, took off his hat, and wiped his forehead. Tension seemed suddenly to relax and his heart for a moment beat thickly; then with a jerk he sat upright. Carmencita was again absorbed in watching the crowds upon the streets, and, when the cab stopped, jumped as if awakened from a dream.

"Are we here already? Oh, my goodness! There she is!"

Miss Barbour was going in the doorway, and as Van Landing saw the straight, slender figure, caught the turn of the head, held in the way that was hers alone, the years that were gone slipped out of memory and she was his again. His - With a swift movement he was out of the cab and on the street and about to follow her when Carmencita touched him on the arm.

"Let me go first. She doesn't know you're coming. We'll get a table near the door."

The crowd separated them, but through it Carmencita wriggled her way quickly and disappeared. Waiting, Van Landing saw her rush up to Miss Barbour, then slip in a chair at a table whose occupants were leaving, and motion Frances to do the same. As the tired little waitress, after taking off the soiled cloth and putting on a fresh one, went away for necessary equipment Van Landing opened the door and walked in and to the table and held out his hand.

"You would not let me thank you this morning. May I thank you now for -"

"Finding him?" Carmencita leaned halfway over the table, and her big blue eyes looked anxiously at first one and then the other. "He was looking for you, Miss Frances; he'd been looking all day and all night because he'd just heard you were somewhere down here, and he's come to have lunch with us, and - Oh, it's Christmas, Miss Frances, and please tell him - say something, do something! He's been waiting three years, and he can't wait another minute. Gracious! that smells good!"

The savory dish that passed caused a turn in Carmencita's head, and Frances Barbour, looking into the eyes that were looking into hers, held out her hand. At sight of Van Landing her face had colored richly, then the color had left it, leaving it white, and in her eyes was that he had never seen before.

"There is nothing for which to thank me." Her voice with its freshness and sweetness stirred as of old, but it was low. She smiled slightly. "I am very glad you are all right this morning. I did not know you knew our part of the town." Her hand was laid on Carmencita's. "I didn't until I met your little friend. I had never been in it before. I know it now very well."

"And he was so fighting mad because he couldn't see you when I sent the note that he went out, not knowing where he was or how to get back, and when his senses came on again and he tried to find out he couldn't find, and he walked 'most all night and was lost like people in a desert who go round and round. And the next day he walked all day long and 'most froze, and he'd passed Mother McNeil's house a dozen times and didn't know it; and he was chasing Noodles and just leaning against that railing when the cop came and you came. Oh, Miss Frances, it's Christmas! Won't you please make up and - When are we going to eat?"

Miss Barbour's hand closed over Carmencita's twisting ones, and into her face again sprang color; then she laughed. "We are very hungry, Mr. Van Landing. Would you mind sitting down so we can have lunch?"

An hour later Carmencita leaned back in her chair, hands in her lap and eyes closed. Presently one hand went out. "Don't ask me anything for a minute, will you? I've got to think about something. When you're ready to go let me know."

Through the meal Carmencita's flow of words and flow of spirits had saved the silences that fell, in spite of effort, between Van Landing and Miss Barbour, and under the quiet poise so characteristic of her he had seen her breath come unsteadily. Could he make her care for him again? With eyes no longer guarded he looked at her, leaned forward.

"From here," he said, "where are you going?"

"Home. I mean to Mother McNeil's. Carmencita says you and she have done my shopping." She smiled slightly and lifted a glass of water to her lips. "The tree is to be dressed this afternoon, and to-night the children come."

"And I - when can I come?"

"You?" She glanced at Carmencita, who was now sitting with her chin on the back of her chair, arms clasping the latter, watching the strange and fascinating scene of people ordering what they wanted to eat and eating as much of it as they wanted. "I don't know. I am very busy. After Christmas, perhaps."

"You mean for me there is to be no Christmas? Am I to be for ever kept outside, Frances?"

"Outside?" She looked up and away. "I have no home. We are both - outside. To have no home at Christmas is -" Quickly she got up. "We must go. It is getting late, and there is much to do."

For one swift moment she let his eyes hold hers, and in his burned all the hunger of the years of loss; then, taking up her muff, she went toward the door. On the street she hesitated, then held out her hand. "Good-by, Mr. Van Landing. I hope you will have a happy Christmas."

"Do you?" Van Landing opened the cab door. "Get in, please. I will come in another cab." Stooping, he pushed aside some boxes and bundles and made room for Carmencita. "I'll be around at four to help dress the tree. Wait until I come." He nodded to the cabman; then, lifting his hat, he closed the door with a click and, turning, walked away.

"Carmencita! oh, Carmencita!" Into the child's eyes the beautiful ones of her friend looked with sudden appeal, and the usually steady hands held those of Carmencita with frightened force. "What have you done? What have you done?"

"Done?" Carmencita's fingers twisted into those of her beloved, and her laugh was joyous. "Done! Not much yet. I've just begun. Did - did you know you were to have a grand Christmas present, Miss Frances? You are. It's - it's alive!"

CHAPTER XV

The time intervening before his return to help with the tree was spent by Van Landing in a certain establishment where jewels were kept and in telephoning Peterkin; and the orders to Peterkin were many. At four o'clock he was back at Mother McNeil's.

In the double parlor of the old-fashioned house, once the home of wealth and power, the tree was already in place, and around it, in crowded confusion, were boxes and barrels, and bundles and toys, and clothes and shoes, and articles of unknown name and purpose, and for a moment he hesitated. Hands in his pockets, he looked first at Mother McNeil and then at a little lame boy on the floor beside an open trunk, out of which he was taking gaily-colored ornaments and untangling yards of tinsel; and then he looked at Frances, who, with a big apron over her black dress, with its soft white collar open at the throat, was holding a pile of empty stockings in her hands.

"You are just in time, my son." Mother McNeil beamed warmly at the uninvited visitor. "When a man can be of service, it's let him serve, I say, and if you will get that stepladder over there and fix this angel on the top of the tree it will save time. Jenkins has gone for more tinsel and more bread. We didn't intend at first to have sandwiches and chocolate - just candy and nuts and things like that - but it's so cold and snowy Frances thought something good and hot would taste well. You can slice the bread, Mr. Van Landing. Four sandwiches apiece for the boys and three for the girls are what we allow." She looked around. "Hand him that angel, Frances, and show him where to put it. I've got to see about the cakes."

Never having fastened an angel to the top of a tree, for a half-moment Van Landing was uncertain how to go about it, fearing exposure of ignorance and awkwardness; then with a quick movement he was up the ladder and looking down at the girl who was handing him a huge paper doll dressed in the garments supposedly worn by the dwellers of mansions in the sky, and as he took it he laughed.

"This is a very worldly-looking angel. She apparently enjoys the blowing of her trumpet. Stand off, will you, and see if that's right?" Van Landing fastened the doll firmly to the top of the tree. "Does she show well down there?"

It was perfectly natural that he should be here and helping. True, he had never heard of Mother McNeil and her home until two nights before, never had dressed a Christmas tree before, or before gone where he was not asked, but things of that sort no longer mattered. What mattered was that he had found Frances, that it was the Christmas season, and he was at last learning the secret of its hold on human hearts and sympathies. There was no time to talk, but as he looked he watched, with eyes that missed no movement that she made, the fine, fair face that to him was like no other on earth, and, watching, he wondered if she, too, wondered at the naturalness of it all.

The years that had passed since he had seen her had left their imprint. She had known great sorrow, also she had traveled much, and, though about her were the grace and courage of old, there was something else, something of nameless and compelling appeal, and he knew that she, too, knew the loneliness of life.

Quickly they worked, and greater and greater grew the confusion of the continually appearing boxes and bundles, and, knee-deep, Mother McNeil surveyed them, hands on her hips, and once or twice she brushed her eyes.

"It's always the way, my son. If you trust people they will not fail you. When we learn how to understand there will be less hate and more help in the world. Jenkins, bring that barrel of apples and box of oranges over here and get a knife for Mr. Van Landing to cut the bread for the sandwiches. It's time to make them. Matilda, call Abraham in. He can slice the ham and cheese. There must be plenty. Boys are hollow. Frances, have you seen my scissors?"

Out of what seemed hopeless confusion and chaotic jumbling, out of excited coming and going, and unanswered questions, and slamming of doors, and hurried searchings, order at last evolved, and, feeling very much as if he'd been in a football match, Van Landing surveyed the rooms with a sense of personal pride in their completeness. Around the tree, placed between the two front windows, were piled countless packages, each marked, and from the mantelpiece hung a row of bulging stockings, reinforced by huge mounds of the same on the floor, guarded already by old Fetch-It. Holly and cedar gave color and fragrance, and at the uncurtained windows wreaths, hung by crimson ribbons, sent a welcome to the waiting crowd outside.

If he were not here he would be alone, with nothing to do. And Christmas eve alone! He drew in his breath and looked at Frances. In her face was warm, rich color, and her eyes were gay and bright, but she was tired. She would deny it if asked. He did not have to ask. If only he could take her away and let her rest!

She was going up-stairs to change her dress. Half-way up the steps he called her, and, leaning against the rail of the banisters, he looked up at her.

"When you come down I must see you, Frances - and alone. I shall wait here for you."

"I cannot see you alone. There will be no time."

"Then we must make time. I tell you I must see you." Something in her eyes made him hesitate. He must try another way. "Listen, Frances. I want you to do me a favor. There's a young girl in my office, my stenographer, who is to be married to-morrow to my head clerk. She is from a little town very far from here and has no relatives, no intimate friends near enough to go to. She lives in a boarding-house, and she can't afford to go home to be married. I have asked Herrick to bring her to my apartment to-morrow and marry her there. I would like her to have - Carmencita and her father are coming, and I want you to come, too. It would make things nicer for her. Will you come - you and Mother McNeil?"

Over the banisters the beautiful eyes looked down into Van Landing's. Out of them had gone guarding. In them was that which sent the blood in hot surge through his heart. "I would love to come, but I am going out of town to-morrow - going -"

"Home?" In Van Landing's voice was unconcealed dismay. The glow of Christmas, new and warm and sweet, died sharply, leaving him cold and full of fear. "Are you going home?"

She shook her head. "I have no home. That is why I am going away to-morrow. Mother McNeil will have her family here, and I'd be - I'd be an outsider. It's everybody's home day - and when you haven't a home -"

She turned and went a few steps farther on to where the stairs curved, then suddenly she sat down and crumpled up and turned her face to the wall. With leaps that took the steps two at a time Van Landing was beside her.

"Frances!" he said, "Frances!" and in his arms he held her close. "You've found out, too! Thank God, you've found out, too!"

Below, a door opened and some one was in the hall. Quickly

Frances was on her feet. "You must not, must not, Stephen - not here!"

"Goodness gracious! they've done made up."

At the foot of the steps Carmencita, as if paralyzed with delight, stood for a moment, then, shutting tight her eyes, ran back whence she came; at the door she stopped.

"Carmencita! Carmencita!" It was Van Landing's voice. She turned her head. "Come here, Carmencita. I have something to tell you."

Eyes awed and shining, Carmencita came slowly up the steps. Reaching them, with a spring she threw her arms around her dear friend's neck and kissed her lips again and again and again, then held out her hands to the man beside her. "Is - is it to be to-morrow, Mr. Van?"

"It is to be to-morrow, Carmencita."

For a half-moment there was quivering silence; then Van Landing spoke again. "There are some things I must attend to to-night. Early to-morrow I will come for you, Frances, and in Dr. Pierson's church we will be married. Herrick and Miss Davis are coming at one o'clock, and my - wife must be there to receive them. And you, too, Carmencita - you and your father. We are going to have -" Van Landing's voice was unsteady. "We are going to have Christmas at home, Frances. Christmas at home!"

CHAPTER XVI

Lifting herself on her elbow, Carmencita listened. There was no sound save the ticking of the little clock on the mantel. For a moment she waited, then with a swift movement of her hand threw back the covering on the cot, slipped from it, and stood, barefooted, in her nightgown, in the middle of the floor. Head on the side, one hand to her mouth, the other outstretched as if for silence from some one unseen, she raised herself on tiptoe and softly, lightly, crossed the room to the door opening into the smaller room wherein her father slept. Hand on the knob, she listened, and, the soft breathing assuring her he was asleep, she closed the door, gave a deep sigh of satisfaction, and hurried back to the cot, close to which she sat down, put on her stockings, and tied on her feet a pair of worn woolen slippers, once the property of her prudent and practical friend, Miss Cattie Burns. Slipping on her big coat over her gown, she tiptoed to the mantel, lighted the candle upon it, and looked at the clock.

"Half past twelve," she said, "and Father's stocking not filled yet!"

As she got down from the chair on which she had stood to see the hour her foot caught in the ripped hem of her coat. She tripped, and would have fallen had she not steadied herself against the table close to the stove, and as she did so she laughed under her breath.

"Really this kimono is much too long." She looked down on

the loosened hem. "And I oughtn't to wear my best accordion-pleated pale-blue crepe de Chine and shadow lace when I am so busy. But dark-gray things are so unbecoming, and, besides, I may have a good deal of company to-night. The King of Love and the Queen of Hearts may drop in, and I wouldn't have time to change. Miss Lucrecia Beck says I'm going to write a book when I'm big, I'm so fond of making up and of love-things. She don't know I've written one already. If he hadn't happened to be standing on that corner looking so - so - I don't know what, exactly, but so something I couldn't help running down and asking him to come up - I never would have had the day I've had to-day and am going to have to-morrow."

Stooping, she pinned the hem of her coat carefully, then, stretching out her arms, stood on her tiptoes and spun noiselessly round and round. "Can't help it!" she said, as if to some one who objected. "I'm so glad I'm living, so glad I spoke to him, and know him, that I'm bound to let it out. Father says I mustn't speak to strangers; but I'd have to be dead not to talk, and I didn't think about his being a man. He looked so lonely."

With quick movements a big gingham apron was tied over the bulky coat, and, putting the candle on the table in the middle of the room, Carmencita began to move swiftly from cot to cupboard, from chairs to book-shelves, and from behind and under each bundles and boxes of varying sizes were brought forth and arrayed in rows on the little table near the stove. As the pile grew bigger so did her eyes, and in her cheeks, usually without color, two spots burned deep and red. Presently she stood off and surveyed her work and, hands clasped behind, began to count, her head nodding with each number.

"Thirteen big ones and nineteen little ones," she said, "and I don't know a thing that's in one of them. Gracious! this is a nice world to live in! I wonder what makes people so good to me? Mrs. Robinsky brought up those six biggest ones to-night." Lightly her finger was laid on each. "She said they were left with her to be sent up to-morrow morning, but there wouldn't be a thing to send if she waited, as the children kept pinching and poking so to see what was in them. I'd like to punch myself. Noodles gave me that." Her head nodded at a queer-shaped package wrapped in brown paper and tied with green cord. "He paid nineteen cents for it. He told me so. I didn't pay but five for what I gave him. He won't brush his teeth or clean his finger-nails, and I told him I wasn't going to give him a thing if he didn't, but I haven't a bit of hold-out-ness at Christmas. I wonder what's in that?"

Cautiously her hand was laid on a box wrapped in white tissue-paper and tied with red ribbons. "I'll hate to open it and see, it looks so lovely and Christmasy, but if I don't see soon I'll die from wanting to know. It rattled a little when I put it on the table. It's Miss Frances's present, and I know it isn't practical. She's like I am. She don't think Christmas is for plain and useful things. She thinks it's for pleasure and pretty ones. I wonder -" Her hands were pressed to her breast, and on tiptoes she leaned quiveringly toward the table. "I wonder if it could be a new tambourine with silver bells on it! If it is I'll die for joy, I'll be so glad! I broke mine to-night. I shook it so hard when I was dancing after I got home from the tree that - Good gracious! I've caught my foot again! These diamond buckles on my satin slippers are always catching the chiffon ruffles on my petticoats. I oughtn't to wear my best things when I'm busy, but I can't stand ugly ones, even to work in. Mercy! it's one o'clock, and the things for Father's stocking aren't out yet."

Out of the bottom drawer of the old-fashioned chest at the end of the room a box was taken and laid on the floor near the stove, into which a small stick of wood was put noiselessly, and carefully Carmencita sat down beside it. Taking off the top of the box, she lifted first a large-size stocking and held it up.

"I wish I was one hundred children's mother at Christmas and had a hundred stockings to fill! I mean, if I had things to fill them with. But as I'm not a mother, just a daughter, I'm thankful glad I've got a father to fill a stocking for. He's the only child I've got. If he could just see how beautiful and red this apple is, and how yellow this orange, and what a darling little candy harp *this* is, I'd be thankfuler still. But he won't ever see. The doctor said so - said I must be his eyes."

One by one the articles were taken out of the box and laid on the floor; and carefully, critically, each was examined.

"This cravat is an awful color." Carmencita's voice made an effort to be polite and failed. "Mr. Robinsky bought it for father himself and asked me to put it in his stocking, but I hate to put. I'll have to do it, of course, and father won't know the colors, but what on earth made him get a green-and-red plaid? Now listen at me! I'm doing just what Miss Lucrecia does to everything that's sent her. The only pleasure she gets out of her presents is making fun of them and snapping at the people who send them. She's an awful snapper. The Damanarkist sent these cigars. They smell good. He don't believe in Christmas, but he sent Father and me both a present. I hope he'll like the picture-frame I made for his mother's picture. His mother's dead, but he believed in her. She was the only thing he did believe in. A man who don't believe in his mother - Oh, _my_ precious mother!"

With a trembling movement the little locket was taken from the box and opened and the picture in it kissed passionately; then, without warning, the child crumpled up and hot tears fell fast over the quivering face. "I do want you, my mother! Everybody wants a mother at Christmas, and I haven't had one since I was seven. Father tries to fill my stocking, but it isn't a mother-stocking, and I just ache and ache to - to have one like you'd fix. I want -" The words came tremblingly, and presently she sat up.

"Carmencita Bell, you are a baby. Behave - your - self!" With the end of the gingham apron the big blue eyes were wiped. "You can't do much in this world, but you can keep from crying. Suppose Father was to know." Her back straightened and her head went up. "Father isn't ever going to know, and if

I don't fill this stocking it won't be hanging on the end of the mantelpiece when he wakes up. The locket must go in the toe."

CHAPTER XVII

In half an hour the stocking, big and bulging, was hung in its accustomed place, the packages for her father put on a chair by themselves, and those for her left on the table, and as she rearranged the latter something about the largest one arrested her attention, and, stopping, she gazed at it with eyes puzzled and uncertain.

It looked - Cautiously her fingers were laid upon it. Undoubtedly it looked like the box in which had been put the beautiful dark-blue coat she had bought for the little friend of her friend. And that other box was the size of the one the two dresses had been put in; and that was a hat-box, and that a shoe-box, and the sash and beads and gloves and ribbons, all the little things, had been put in a box that size. Every drop of blood surged hotly, tremblingly, and with eyes staring and lips half parted her breath came unsteadily.

In the confusion of their coming she had not noticed when Mrs. Robinsky had brought them up and put them under the cot, with the injunction that they were not to be opened until the morning, and for the first time their familiarity was dawning on her. Could it be - could *she* be the little friend he had said was rich? She wasn't rich. He didn't mean money-rich, but she wasn't any kind of rich; and she had been so piggy.

Hot color swept over her face, and her hands twitched. She had told him again and again she was getting too much, but he

KATE LANGLEY BOSHER

had insisted on her buying more, and made her tell him what little girls liked, until she would tell nothing more. And they had all been for her. For her, Carmencita Bell, who had never heard of him three days before.

In the shock of revelation, the amazement of discovery, the little figure at the table stood rigid and upright, then it relaxed and with a stifled sob Carmencita crossed the room and, by the side of her cot, twisted herself into a little knot and buried her face in her arms and her arms in the covering.

"I didn't believe! I didn't believe!"

Over and over the words came tremblingly. "I prayed and prayed, but I didn't believe! He let it happen, and I didn't believe!"

For some moments there were queer movements of twitching hands and twisting feet by the side of the cot, but after a while a tear-stained, awed, and shy-illumined face looked up from the arms in which it had been hidden and ten slender fingers intertwined around the knees of a hunched-up little body, which on the floor drew itself closer to the fire.

It was a wonderful world, this world in which she lived. Carmencita's eyes were looking toward the window, through which she could see the shining stars. Wonderful things happened in it, and quite beyond explaining were these things, and there was no use trying to understand. Two days ago she was just a little girl who lived in a place she hated and was too young to go to work, and who had a blind father and no rich friends or relations, and there was nothing nice that could happen just so.

"But things don't happen just so. They happen - don't anybody know how, I guess." Carmencita nodded at the stars. "I've prayed a good many times before and nothing happened, and I don't know why all this beautifulness should have come to me, and Mrs. Beckwith, who is good as gold, though a poor manager with babies, shouldn't ever have any luck. I don't understand, but I'm awful thankful. I wish I could let God know, and the Christ-child know, how thankful I am. Maybe the way they'd like me to tell is by doing something nice for somebody else. I know. I'll ask Miss Parker to supper Christmas night. She's an awful poky person and needs new teeth, but she says she's so sick of mending pants, she wishes some days she was dead. And I'll ask the Damanarkist. He hasn't anywhere to go, and he hates rich people so it's ruined his stomach. Hate is an awful ruiner."

For some moments longer Carmencita sat in huddled silence, then presently she spoke again.

"I didn't intend to give Miss Cattie Burns anything. I've tried to like Miss Cattie and I can't. But it was very good in her to send us a quarter of a cord of wood for a Christmas present. She can't help being practical. I'll take her that red geranium to-morrow. I raised it from a slip, and I hate to see it go, but it's all I've got to give. It will have to go.

"And to-morrow. I mean to-day - this is Christmas day! Oh, a happy Christmas, everybody!" Carmencita's arms swung out, then circled swiftly back to her heart. "For everybody in all the world I'd make it happy if I could! And I'm going to a wedding to-day - a wedding! I don't wonder you're thrilly, Carmencita Bell!"

For a half-moment breath came quiveringly from the parted lips, then again at the window and the stars beyond the little head nodded.

"But I'll never wonder at things happening any more. I'll just wonder at there being so many nice people on this earth. All are not nice. The Damanarkist says there is a lot of rot in them, a lot of meanness and cheatingness, and nasty people who don't want other people to do well or to get in their way; but there's bound to be more niceness than nastiness, or the world couldn't go on. It couldn't without a lot of love. It takes a lot of love to stand life. I read that in a book. Maybe that's why we have Christmas - why the Christ-child came."

Shyly the curly head was bent on the upraised knees, and the palms of two little hands were uplifted. "O God, all I've got to give is love. Help me never to forget, and put a lot in my heart so I'll always have it ready. And I thank You and thank You for letting such grand things happen. I didn't dream there'd really be a marriage when I asked You please to let it be if you could manage it; but there's going to be two, and I'm going to both. I've got a new dress to wear, and slippers with buckles, and amber beads, and lots of other things. And most of all I thank You for Mr. Van and Miss Frances finding each other. And please don't let them ever lose each other again. They might, even if they are married, if they don't take care. Please help them to take care, for Christ's sake. Amen."

* * * * *

On her feet, Carmencita patted the stocking hanging from the mantel, took off the big coat, kicked the large, loose slippers across the room, blew out the candle, and stood for a moment poised on the tip of her toes.

"If I could" - the words came breathlessly - "if I could I'd dance like the lady I was named for, but it might wake Father. I mustn't wake Father. Good night, everybody - and a merry Christmas to all this nice, big world!"

With a spring that carried her across the room Carmencita was on her cot and beneath its covering, which she drew up to her face. Under her breath she laughed joyously, and her arms were hugged to her heart.

"To-morrow - I mean to-day - I am going to tell them. They don't understand yet. They think it was just an accident." She shook her head. "It wasn't an accident. After they're married I'm going to tell them. Tell them how it happened."

Choose from Thousands of 1stWorldLibrary Classics By

Adolphus William Ward
Aesop
Agatha Christie
Alexander Aaronsohn
Alexander Kielland
Alexandre Dumas
Alfred Gatty
Alfred Ollivant
Alice Duer Miller
Alice Turner Curtis
Alice Dunbar
Ambrose Bierce
Amelia E. Barr
Andrew Lang
Andrew McFarland Davis
Anna Sewell
Annie Besant
Annie Hamilton Donnell
Annie Payson Call
Anton Chekhov
Arnold Bennett
Arthur Conan Doyle
Arthur Ransome
Atticus
B. M. Bower
Basil King
Bayard Taylor
Ben Macomber
Booth Tarkington
Bram Stoker
C. Collodi
C. E. Orr
C. M. Ingleby
Carolyn Wells
Catherine Parr Traill
Charles A. Eastman
Charles Dickens
Charles Dudley Warner
Charles Farrar Browne
Charles Ives
Charles Kingsley
Charles Lathrop Pack
Charles Whibley
Charles Willing Beale
Charlotte M. Braeme
Charlotte M. Yonge
Clair W. Hayes
Clarence Day Jr.
Clarence E. Mulford

Clemence Housman
Confucius
Cornelis DeWitt Wilcox
Cyril Burleigh
D. H. Lawrence
Daniel Defoe
David Garnett
Don Carlos Janes
Donald Keyhole
Dorothy Kilner
Dougan Clark
E. Nesbit
E.P.Roe
E. Phillips Oppenheim
Edgar Allan Poe
Edgar Rice Burroughs
Edith Wharton
Edward J. O'Biren
John Cournos
Edwin L. Arnold
Eleanor Atkins
Elizabeth Cleghorn
Gaskell
Elizabeth Von Arnim
Ellem Key
Emily Dickinson
Erasmus W. Jones
Ernie Howard Pie
Ethel Turner
Ethel Watts Mumford
Eugenie Foa
Eugene Wood
Evelyn Everett-Green
Everard Cotes
F. J. Cross
Federick Austin Ogg
Ferdinand Ossendowski
Francis Bacon
Francis Darwin
Frances Hodgson Burnett
Frank Gee Patchin
Frank Harris
Frank Jewett Mather
Frank L. Packard
Frederick Trevor Hill
Frederick Winslow Taylor
Friedrich Kerst
Friedrich Nietzsche
Fyodor Dostoyevsky

Gabrielle E. Jackson
Garrett P. Serviss
Gaston Leroux
George Ade
Geroge Bernard Shaw
George Ebers
George Eliot
George MacDonald
George Orwell
George Tucker
George W. Cable
George Wharton James
Gertrude Atherton
Grace E. King
Grant Allen
Guillermo A. Sherwell
Gulielma Zollinger
Gustav Flaubert
H. A. Cody
H. B. Irving
H. G. Wells
H. H. Munro
H. Irving Hancock
H. Rider Haggard
H. W. C. Davis
Hamilton Wright Mabie
Hans Christian Andersen
Harold Avery
Harold McGrath
Harriet Beecher Stowe
Harry Houidini
Helent Hunt Jackson
Helen Nicolay
Hendy David Thoreau
Henrik Ibsen
Henry Adams
Henry Ford
Henry Frost
Henry James
Henry Jones Ford
Henry Seton Merriman
Henry Wadsworth
Longfellow
Henry W Longfellow
Herbert A. Giles
Herbert N. Casson
Herman Hesse
Homer
Honore De Balzac

Horace Walpole	Laurence Housman	Robert Lansing
Horatio Alger, Jr.	Leo Tolstoy	Robert Michael Ballantyne
Howard Pyle	Leonid Andreyev	Robert W. Chambers
Howard R. Garis	Lewis Carroll	Rosa Nouchette Carey
Hugh Lofting	Lilian Bell	Ross Kay
Hugh Walpole	Lloyd Osbourne	Rudyard Kipling
Humphry Ward	Louis Tracy	Samuel B. Allison
Ian Maclaren	Louisa May Alcott	Samuel Hopkins Adams
Israel Abrahams	Lucy Fitch Perkins	Sarah Bernhardt
J.G.Austin	Lucy Maud Montgomery	Selma Lagerlof
J. Henri Fabre	Lydia Miller Middleton	Sherwood Anderson
J. M. Barrie	Lyndon Orr	Sigmund Freud
J. Macdonald Oxley	M. H. Adams	Standish O'Grady
J. S. Knowles	Margaret E. Sangster	Stanley Weyman
J. Storer Clouston	Margaret Vandercook	Stella Benson
Jack London	Maria Edgeworth	Stephen Crane
Jacob Abbott	Maria Thompson Daviess	Stewart Edward White
James Allen	Mariano Azuela	Stijn Streuvels
James Lane Allen	Marion Polk Angellotti	Swami Abhedananda
James Andrews	Mark Overton	Swami Parmananda
James Baldwin	Mark Twain	T. S. Ackland
James DeMille	Mary Austin	The Princess Der Ling
James Joyce	Mary Cole	Thomas A. Janvier
James Oliver Curwood	Mary Rowlandson	Thomas A Kempis
James Oppenheim	Mary Wollstonecraft	Thomas Anderton
James Otis	Shelley	Thomas Bailey Aldrich
Jane Austen	Max Beerbohm	Thomas Bulfinch
Jens Peter Jacobsen	Myra Kelly	Thomas De Quincey
Jerome K. Jerome	Nathaniel Hawthrone	Thomas H. Huxley
John Burroughs	O. F. Walton	Thomas Hardy
John F. Kennedy	Oscar Wilde	Thomas More
John Gay	Owen Johnson	Thornton W. Burgess
John Glasworthy	P.G.Wodehouse	U. S. Grant
John Habberton	Paul and Mable Thorn	Valentine Williams
John Joy Bell	Paul G. Tomlinson	Victor Appleton
John Milton	Paul Severing	Virginia Woolf
John Philip Sousa	Peter B. Kyne	Walter Scott
Jonathan Swift	Plato	Washington Irving
Joseph Carey	R. Derby Holmes	Wilbur Lawton
Joseph Conrad	R. L. Stevenson	Wilkie Collins
Joseph Jacobs	Rabindranath Tagore	Willa Cather
Julian Hawthrone	Rahul Alvares	Willard F. Baker
Julies Vernes	Ralph Waldo Emmerson	William Makepeace
Justin Huntly McCarthy	Rene Descartes	Thackeray
Kakuzo Okakura	Rex E. Beach	William W. Walter
Kenneth Grahame	Richard Harding Davis	Winston Churchill
Kate Langley Bosher	Richard Jefferies	Yei Theodora Ozaki
L. A. Abbot	Robert Barr	Young E. Allison
L. T. Meade	Robert Frost	Zane Grey
L. Frank Baum	Robert Gordon Anderson	
Laura Lee Hope	Robert L. Drake